I0592886

The Radiant King

Reed Lavender: 2

Ashley Capes

The Radiant King
(Reed Lavender: 2)
Copyright © 2020 by Ashley Capes

Cover: Illustration by Vivid Covers
Layout & Typeset: Close-Up Books

ISBN-978-0-6487704-2-8

www.ashleycapes.com

Published by Close-Up Books
Melbourne, Australia

For Brooke

Chapter 1.

Duong was waiting in a navy suit out the front of Reed's apartment building when he returned from the underground, knucklebone in pocket. The detective leant against the old stone walls. Shades cloaked his eyes from the afternoon sun, not that it was truly that bright.

Maybe he's hung over.

Cigarette butts covered the Coke can he held and his suit jacket was a little rumpled but he straightened with a nod. "So, let's talk inside."

"About SEDO?"

"Right."

Reed led Duong inside and then onto the elevator, where they travelled in silence. Duong was now chewing gum – the smell of mint strong. *Probably best I don't ask him how the quitting thing is going, then.*

Once inside, Reed took Duong to the kitchen and opened the fridge. "Drink?"

"I'm fine, Reed."

He lifted some milk free and poured a tall glass.

"That lot at SEDO claim that you were the last to see Petros Martin alive," Duong began. "What can you tell me?"

Treveyos' real name, no doubt. "That he's probably a con artist like the rest of them."

"I'm doing this here instead of in an interrogation room as a courtesy, you know."

Reed raised his hands. "Sorry, I realise that." He took a long drink of his milk. How much truth exactly could he afford to share? He gestured to the bruising at his throat. "I asked a few questions about Garibaldi and Elise. It got heated actually, and he attacked me. I guess I passed out but when I woke up he was gone."

"Right." Doung started writing.

"Right."

He glanced up from his notes. "Those hippies claim you drugged them."

Reed sighed. "Then have them take any test you like; nothing will show up because I didn't drug them."

"Then what did you do?"

"Nothing," Reed replied, and it wasn't a lie so he didn't need to try to sell it. "I didn't see either of them on my way home, which is where I went right after."

"Time?"

"Can't really remember, to be honest. Morning though."

"And earlier today?"

"Meaning?"

"What were you doing in the underground?"

Reed leaned forward. "Did you have me followed?"

"You bet I did," he snapped. "Listen, you're someone I have to watch now, whether you like it or not. And it's obvious that *something* is going on with this Petros Martin guy and I want to know what it has to do with you and the case we're supposedly working on together."

"Shit, are you saying you think I killed him?"

He pointed his pen at Reed. "What I think is that you're not telling me everything; it's pretty simple."

"Then tell *me* something – have you checked this Petros guy out? You find anything linking him to Garibaldi or Dunstall?"

The sharp ring of a mobile cut Duong's answer off. "Yeah?" His voice was terse. Then his expression grew a little less agitated, and he turned his back to cross the room, heading for the door. "You serious?"

Reed followed.

Whoever was on the other line kept talking a little longer, then Duong hung up and turned around again. He jammed his phone into a pocket then tore a cigarette from a pack, though he didn't light it yet.

"What's going on?"

"That was someone we both know – Officer Huggins. He tells me that Petros Martin apparently filed a harassment report against you just now."

Reed frowned. Treveyos was *definitely* dead before any such report had been filed.

"Well, I'm sure it won't come to anything," Duong said as he started for the door, still appearing at least somewhat agitated. "Probably not with those bruises of yours – but I'm going to follow up with Mr Martin now, and you're not invited."

"Fine," Reed said. "But press him about –"

Duong shook his head, already in the short hallway leading to the door. "Don't tell me how to do this, Reed. And we're going to talk again and when we do, I want whatever it is that you're holding back." The door slammed behind him.

Reed slumped back in his chair. *A stay of execution?*

The creak of his fridge seal being broken echoed from the kitchen. "You've only got milk and juice again. Is that any way to thank me?" a voice called.

Max.

Reed found the man with his torso half in the fridge. As ever, Max wore jeans and leather jacket and when he turned, he had his aviator sunglasses on. No scarf today, however. "Don't you have any vodka or something?"

"That'd be in the freezer if I did."

"So, that's a no, right?"

"Very good, cousin," Reed replied with a smile. "I'm guessing you came here to harvest some gratitude?"

"Of course. You should have seen my Treveyos impression. Nailed the voice too."

He chuckled. "Well, I do owe you now."

"Plus the time we stole that jumping castle."

"I remember."

"Well, I'll set it aside for now – gentleman that I am, so we can get started on this hand hunt."

"I don't know."

"Well, it's another order-poorly-disguised-as-a-request from Mother, so let's get cracking."

"Lina didn't tell you about the knuckle bone?"

Max removed his sunglasses, revealing dark eyes. "I was hoping to distract you with work, to be honest. She said Pluto didn't have much to offer."

"Not really."

"Then maybe we should get to work finding Feronia's missing hand, now that she's letting her fingers do the walking."

"What?"

"You know, that ad for phone books. Do humans still use phone books?"

Reed rubbed at his neck. "Max, do you have any idea of what year it is on our calendar?"

He spread his hands. "Fine. Some people do, yes. And yes, nice pun there."

"I was hoping you'd tell me as much."

Reed groaned as he rubbed at his neck. "So, you really think we'll find something?"

"Of course."

"Your optimism is dazzling," Reed replied. "What have you got in mind?"

"I think we should visit an old timer, someone who'd have an ear to the ground." Max was smiling.

"What does that mean?"

"Just go where I tell you. I don't want to ruin the surprise."

"Fine." Reed collected his things and headed out, striding toward the elevator. It was blessedly empty again, not that anyone would have seen Max in any event. At the bottom, Reed paused as a figure crossed the lobby. It was his neighbour Steve, his easy-going expression missing as he hailed the desk clerk.

"Trouble?" Max asked.

Reed shrugged. "I dunno, he looks a little agitated is all. He's one of my neighbours."

Max raised an eyebrow. "Nice of you to worry about the other humans."

Reed jabbed at his cousin with his car keys, but Max skipped out of reach. "Tell me where we're going already."

"A nursery in the suburb of Hawthorn."

"Why?"

"Don't make me spoil it."

***

The Growing Bud Nursery stood just outside of Hawthorn. Out front, a lush row of plants, flowers and pots, and the rich scent of earth and fertiliser. They approached, passing a young family on the footpath.

Max took Reed past lines of succulents and sprouts and furniture and finally to a dusty collection of garden gnomes – most with AFL colours or the classic blue tunic and red hat. All motionless concrete. "Here."

"Where?"

Max gestured to the gnomes.

"So, who's your friend, Max?" Reed asked, keeping his voice low despite the lack of other customers.

"David." Max sat before the row of gnomes, crossing his legs. "David, are you there?"

Reed crossed his arms. "His name is David? As in, *David the Gnome?*"

"That's how he's introduced himself in the past."

"But it's a kid's show from the 1980s. This is a joke, right?"

Max snorted. "No – that's his name. And the cartoon you're thinking of was a book series first. Wil Huygen. He was Dutch."

"Ah, how silly of me."

Max glanced over his shoulder with a wink. "Come on, let me distract you with trivia. I have a third thing for when the time is right, you know."

Reed groaned. "What do you think David will know?"

"Maybe nothing, but I want to ask. Ah, here he comes."

The nearest gnome, a little taller than the others, legs swinging from a toadstool, twitched and then the eyes blinked, focusing on Max first. "You again?"

"Hello David. You look like you're having fun."

"Do I? Well, this model's got that whimsical look, you know, but I'd rather this one I found over in Toorak. The guy hides it from his neighbours. It's part minotaur or something and when I take it out for a stroll it scares the shit out of the other stats."

"Stats?" The question came out before Reed could stop it.

"*Statues*, obviously. Who are you? I see you're not quite as dead as Max here, are you?"

"Not really, no."

Max chuckled. "Ah, David. We're hoping you've noticed something since you spend a lot of time with your feet on the earth, something went missing and we can't find it."

"That business with Feronia?"

"Right."

"Yeah, I felt her hand – it went tearing across the state a little while ago. It disappeared right in the city, about the State Library I'd say."

"You could feel it?"

The gnome snorted. "Of course – well, up until that point. Then it disappeared. So, will that be all, gentlemen?"

Max stood. "Yes, thank you, David. That's a big help."

"Yeah, yeah."

The eyes closed.

Chapter 2.

The afternoon sun peeked between heavy clouds, shining on the green lawns that lay before the State Library. And while no-one really lounged about upon it like they might have in summer, people were meeting on the glistening steps and between the columns, some with dark umbrellas at their sides.

Breath steamed where they spoke, coffees in hand.

Reed glanced at Max, who was rubbing at his sunglasses with his white t-shirt. "Are you sure we can trust David about this?"

"I am."

"Who is he, really – you've been holding out all the way over here but I think I need to know before we go nosing about in there."

"Worried about running into that young lady again... what was her name? You know, one of Minerva's girls. Emily? No, Emma, right?"

He exhaled. "No, that's not the problem, cousin. In fact, Aunty suggested visiting Minerva anyway."

"Convincing," Max said with a grin. "And by the way, it's going to be 'you' not 'we' because I've got another lead I'm going to follow up on; Mother's calling us."

"Fine. But you still haven't answered my question."

"David is probably the last servant of one of those Anglo-Norman deities that Vanished over the centuries. Happy?"

"Hmmm. So, when will you be back?"

"I'm not sure – Mother was hinting that she had been told by Jupiter to keep us all on a shorter leash."

"Leash?"

"Charming, isn't it?" Max said.

"I sincerely hope that means she doesn't expect me to hunt down the thief by myself now. I'm a little tired of doing that sort of thing alone."

"No. Everyone's worried about that. I think Jupiter is more concerned about the rules when we go snooping about in people's homes and offices for you."

"Ah." Which meant getting a hold of Dunstall would have to happen via more conventional means. *And considering Duong's current mood, that's not going to be easy.* A quick flight to Malaysia was hardly on the cards either. *And I don't think I can go into debt with any more deities at this point, since I bloody well owe people all over town.*

"Look, just see if you and Minerva's girl can come up with anything at the library while I'm gone. If the trail disappeared here, it disappeared for a reason."

"Right – but if so, shouldn't Minerva or Emma have told someone about it by now?"

Max frowned. "That's true." Then he shrugged, blinking out of sight, though his voice lingered. "All the more reason to investigate. Be careful too."

"Shit."

Going in there *was* a bit of a problem if Emma still worked for the library. And not because things had ended poorly; it was a pretty regular break-up. She instigated it and eventually, he came to terms. That was it.

Or so you like to tell yourself.

Reed crossed the lawn and skipped a few steps on his way up to the open doors, crossing the foyer and heading through the tables beneath the massive white dome, then for the archives where he found Emma, typing away at her desk.

Emma looked up from her computer, hands hovering above the keyboard. Her dark hair was cut short now; it suited her too. Equally dark eyes regarded him with surprise and... a hint of worry? *That doesn't make sense, does it?*

She stood to move around her desk, black skirt and blouse typical of her style, and pulled him close for a quick hug. "This day just got even more interesting," she said, a faint trace of her Greek accent lingering.

"I feel the same."

She gestured to the chair opposite her own. "I bet I can guess why you're here too." She lowered her voice. "Feronia?"

"Then you felt it?"

She nodded. "Actually, I can show you."

Emma took him from her office to a long corridor that eventually led down to a heavy-looking security door. She waved a card at the security panel then pushed the door open with both hands.

Light flickered on, transforming looming shadows into

shelves of books; all exceptionally neat save for the variety in heights, but the depth of each spine was aligned to an almost inhumanly even degree.

"I see your subtle touch down here," he said.

"Very funny," she said, a hand on her hip. She still wore her silver and gold threaded ring, a gift from her father. "Well, do you see it?"

He did. Grey patches covered the floor, like tears in the very world, the Fringe seeping through but remaining quite... localised. The patches seemed to hop further into the archive, deeper and deeper past the 'general' and reference books until stopping before a large, glass display case where a mediaeval manuscript stood, open to a page that showed a white tower being constructed.

A Book of Hours.

It should have been quite fancifully illuminated, rare as it was, but the pages stood grey and lifeless.

"This is the point from which the hand disappeared," Emma said, expression troubled.

"Via this book?"

"Yes. As though it actually climbed the Tower of Babel."

Reed folded his arms. "That's... quite the omen."

"It's no more rare or special than the few other mediaeval manuscripts we house here. The page was at random. I cannot trace it from here, nor can Minerva."

"You've tried?"

Emma shook her head. "Stupid question, isn't it?"

"True. I kinda wished you'd told us about it."

"I told Minerva – I assume she told the others." Now she smiled. "And what makes you think your family is in charge of dealing with what happened?"

"I got that impression from Aunty."

"Did you?" She chuckled. "Well, whether it's true or not I suppose you're here now. Want my thoughts?"

"Very much."

"I think we're dealing with something sophisticated – obviously, but also something *old*."

"How old?"

"Maybe before our Pantheon."

Reed blinked. *That* was old indeed. But who and why? He nearly groaned; it sounded like fresh, relentless trouble. Just what Jupiter wanted him to face, so maybe it shouldn't have been a surprise. "What leads you that way?"

"Aside from the exit point, take a look. Can you read anything?"

"Well, my Latin is pretty good so..." he trailed off. The words were not written in Latin at all – instead, kanji characters were visible. He glanced back to Emma, who merely pointed once more. The flowing yet 'dotted' script of Arabic now rested on the crumbling paper. He blinked and now it was Latin once more, yet quickly it became something else – vaguely Nordic.

"It has been thus for me ever since the hand touched it," she explained.

"No-one else sees it?"

"No. But I don't think it's an error for the very page that features Babel to appear like this."

Reed exhaled. "Got any ideas then? Are you thinking Sumerian?"

"Maybe. How about you give me a bit more time to look into this, then take me to dinner and we'll talk again."

"That sounds like a date."

She shook her head. "Or maybe I'm just going to be hungry once I finish up."

"Prudent of you to plan your meals so far ahead," Reed replied.

"I know. Now, I'd better get you out of here, since this place is off limits to the public."

Chapter 3.

"He does need the files today, yeah," Reed said, affecting a gentler tone as he paced the street before the library, mobile in hand. Surprisingly, the sun had more or less taken over the sky, but it was not warm. The footpaths were not crowded at least, this far from any cafe.

"You can't just e-mail them?" Sarah replied, her long-suffering-secretary tone evident.

"'fraid not, the boss wants it hand-delivered to ensure it's received; it wouldn't do for the Crown to be accused of being derelict in their duty when it comes to informing the defence of this new development."

Sarah sighed. "Fine. He's at the *Pinto* in Carlton, I'm sure if you hurry you'll catch him."

"Thank you, that helps a lot."

Reed hung up with a grin. Finally, he had the location of Dunstall's solicitor. The snake had proven rather difficult to pin down, and formal requests for a meeting had of course been blown off or deferred with platitudes.

Which left me with deception.

Reed strode down a few blocks to where his car waited, double-parked in a quiet side street lined with the allergy-rich plane trees. He did a quick circuit of the vehicle. He'd gotten away with being a bit of a jerk for now; no tickets and no scratches.

He hopped inside and fired the engine, flicking the radio off as he pulled into the mob of traffic. The flow oozed its way toward the city centre – though he ducked out of the rows of vehicles before they became too disgusting, heading for *Pinto*.

But he'd barely made it out of the traffic and into a quiet side street to search for the mythical empty parking spot, the lines of shops switching to jammed town-houses of old concrete, when something erupted from the street.

Reed slammed the brakes on.

It was a large golden shape, easily seven feet tall and covered in fur, claws swinging as it sprinted down the road... werewolf! Was it Devin? *Why's he taking such a stupid risk?* The werewolf leapt over a modest garden wall and then, moments later, a man dressed in singlet and jeans vaulted the fence, walking away with a couple of backward glances.

Cracked asphalt and dirt lay strewn about the road. One nearby car now sported a shattered passenger window, others with dents from flying debris. And now Reed couldn't drive any further either; the hole was just too big.

He leapt out and charged after the werewolf, feet pounding along the footpath – Devin had turned a corner and was already out of sight. Something was wrong if the man was willing to take such a risk – there was a chance his natural camouflage would confuse any possible witnesses into thinking they'd only seen a large dog... but the giant hole in the road was something else.

Reed skidded around the corner –

Hands slapped around his shoulders, and then he was swung up against the side of a house with a thump. Devin's hazel eyes were suddenly very close, rage fading when he recognised him. "Reed?"

"Hello, Devin."

The man let go. "What the hell are you doing following me?"

"You kind of exploded out of the street."

The man rubbed at the stubble on his chin. "Yeah, well I was taking a bit of a shortcut and something started chasing me. I *think* I lost it."

"When you burst out of the street?"

He nodded. "I don't think it liked the light."

Reed glanced around the corner, back to the hole and his car. Things underground that didn't enjoy light was no small list at all... but it if bothered someone like Devin –

A mighty crack echoed up the street.

"Shit." Another slab of the road had collapsed, near enough to his Ford that it began to roll forward. "Shit!" The car slid down into the hole, crunching to a halt, half-sunken now.

"Define 'unlucky', right?" Devin asked.

Reed glowered at him. "Hilarious. Any ideas about whatever was chasing you?"

"Not much, just that it was shadowy and that it had a strange scent... I can't quite place it." He shrugged. "Anyway, like I said, it didn't like the light and I'd better keep on."

"Wait," Reed said, glancing away from his car again. "Have you heard about the recent trouble?"

"Who hasn't?"

"So, I guess you didn't see the hand or anything?"

Devin shook his shaggy head. "No, sorry."

"Thanks."

"Good luck with your car, mate," he said as he loped off.

Reed turned back to the slowly gathering crowd, most folks sticking to their yards or front windows, many whipping out their phones to take pictures. *Yes, immortalise my shitty luck, everyone.*

He crossed the street and jogged to his Falcon, testing the footing around the gaping hole and the debris that kept his car approximately 'above' ground. Inside, he had a few vaguely personal possessions but perhaps nothing so valuable that he had to worry about people robbing him – and so he stared within the open hole instead.

No hints of movement, just dark earth, crumbled asphalt and the gleam of pipes.

What had Devin encountered?

It could have been at least a dozen things – but if the wolf couldn't identify the scent, did that suggest something new? Or was it a possible taint from Feronia's influence? Too many possibilities. Reed pulled out his mobile and dialled for emergency services, explained what had happened and then began to pace, declining well-meaning offers of help from a few of the residents as he found a tree to lean against, the bark cold against his back.

Not having a car for who knew how long was going to be a problem.

And not just because of public transport. Or, more accurately, certain members of the public who appeared on that transport. And more seriously, if one of his obligations ended up some way out of the city then he'd be in trouble. *Worse, it's hard to chase down a fleeing suspect with a tram.*

Pinto's will have to wait too.

Lina popped into existence across the road, then grinned as she skipped over to him, her skirt twirling. The hem had been embroidered with cartoon characters for some reason. "How did you manage that?" she asked.

"I have no idea." He explained what had happened, and the news from Devin.

"It's odd that he didn't recognise it," she said with a frown, her blue lips pursed. "I have news in the meantime."

"Good news?"

"Just 'news' I suppose. Potter wants to speak with you."

"Then you were wrong; that's bad news, Lina."

She sighed. "It could be important."

"But not important enough for him to come himself."

"My guess is he asked me because you'd be more inclined to listen – because I'm your favourite, of course," she said with a grin. "Max thinks it's him but we know better, right?"

Reed hung his head. "Where is he then?"

She lowered her voice. "Working the car parks of pokie venues."

"Oh." Reed glanced away. *That* probably meant only one thing... one very, very bad thing. His stomach flipped. "Can you ask him to visit me later tonight?"

"Oooh, got a date, do you?"

"So, you've spoken to Emma already, I take it."

"I might have popped in to the library; you know, to follow up on the idea of speaking to Minerva."

"You mean, to fish for gossip, since I'm sure you knew

that I've already been there."

Lina winked at him as she twirled away, disappearing gradually, her voice lingering when she was gone. "Spoilsport."

And the meal with Emma, while no date, certainly did have him a little apprehensive and equally excited... but Potter's request was a real dampener.

What did the old sourpuss want now?

Chapter 4.

Reed waited in the Italian restaurant with its soft tablecloths, stunning photography of distant cities and coastlines, and Lucio Battisti on the sound system. Pots of red and pink geraniums sat on the table, perhaps an odd choice and yet during winter maybe the restaurant had limited options. He nearly called one of the sleek waiters over to remove them, in case they signalled a romantic dinner – but Emma appeared, weaving her way through the clinking of cutlery and the other diners in their neat clothing.

He stared a moment; she did embody the sexy librarian look – only, not the cliché where the woman removed her glasses or let her hair down to 'transform', she looked great without changing anything.

He couldn't squash a memory of lying in bed with her, the softness of the skin...

"You know, Reed," she said as she sat down, placing her handbag on an unused chair. "You could have met me out front. Your legs aren't broken are they?"

"They're fine so far," he replied.

"I was going to pay for our meal myself, you know. If you're not too proud, that is."

"I'd really appreciate that, actually," he said without a trace of sarcasm.

She chuckled. "That's one of the reasons things didn't work for you and me."

"My ability to accept the generosity of those around me?"

"No."

"Ah. My *need* to accept the generosity of those around me?"

"No, Reed." Her smile had faded. "I know you'd do anything for your friends and you pay everyone back anything you owe the second you can… it's just that I don't want to feel like I have a little brother to take care of."

He scratched at his cheek. "Well, that's pretty clear."

She patted his other hand, expression softening. "That sounded worse than I meant it to sound, actually."

"Good to know," Reed said. "Because I'm actually older than you."

She laughed. "Okay, funny guy, nice deflection. I didn't actually mean to unload that on you, honest. But I guess I was thinking about us on the way here."

"I tried not to," he said. "But I think I will *afterwards* now."

"Well, how about we switch things back to a professional setting?"

"Can do," he said, though he kept a faint sense of disappointment hidden. "So, what do you think happened?"

She lowered her voice a little, though their conversation probably sounded rather academic to any incidental eavesdroppers. "The languages on the manuscript keep changing but thankfully, not just anyone can see that. There's no pattern but I did notice that an unfamiliar phrase seems to be repeated, no matter the language."

Before he could answer, the waiter appeared to take their order – he took the ravioli in Napoletana sauce and she a creamy fettuccini.

Once the fellow was gone, Reed looked to her once more. "So, was something missing from the 'book of hours' then?"

"It was. I first noticed it during the Sumerian," she said, then raised an eyebrow; it seemed, in order to add a little drama to the moment. "Okay, so, are you ready? It's a little odd."

"I'm even more interested, if possible," he said, taking a drink from his water.

"Good – and keep in mind, I've translated this to make it a little more interesting, but the same phrase that appears each time is 'all work and no play makes Jack a dull boy'."

"Ah..."

"Told you."

Reed lowered his glass. "You did."

"I assume it is meant to be from the proverb, rather than *The Shining*," she said with a grin.

"That's... not what I was expecting, to be honest. Is that really what it says?"

"More or less. More literally, I think it's closer to 'enough is enough, others must work now for I have earned my fun', and even that is beyond odd."

"So, are you saying you believe that those words are essentially a message left behind by Feronia's missing hand?"

She shrugged. "Not really. I'm saying that after the hand mauled my manuscript that the phrase appeared."

"Good, some clarity at last."

She kicked him under the table. "Just remember who's helping you now, Reed. It's a starting point."

"No, it is. And I'd have nothing without what you've given me, Emma." *But what* did *it mean?* Was the hand even more sentient or was it whoever lurked behind the event, the power that Jupiter had warned about? And if so, did the thing have a sense of humour?

Or a sense of bitterness?

"I'll keep reading and see what else I can discover," she said. "How about you?"

Reed leaned back in the chair. "I don't know anymore. Obviously I'd love to figure out where the hand *went* but I doubt I could follow. I think for now, my only other option is to chase down one of the Shining Leaves – at least two of them got away. Maybe they know some way to locate the Hand?"

"That's probably worth looking into. So, where will you start?"

"Their old office. Or maybe the casino."

She took a bite of her own meal; fettuccini. "Yeah?"

"I think there's a link between them and a murdering drug-lord I'm after. Supposedly he's got a suite there."

She frowned at him. "You're not getting in over your head, are you?"

"No more than usual, I suppose."

"You know you have to stay alive long enough for me to actually find and then give you information."

"I'm not rushing in to anything. I'll do some research first," he said, then smiled. "So, where did we land on dessert? Because I was thinking, when the waiter comes back I think we should order. I haven't had a good pannacotta for ages."

***

Reed slipped through his door before midnight, flicking on lights as he made his way to the kitchen. There, he pulled open the fridge then poured his usual glass of milk. He took it to the lounge and slumped into a chair, flicking the television on with a sigh. Emma *had* paid for dinner in the end, which was indeed welcome, before driving him home and leaving with a promise to deliver anything else she could come up with.

Which only left Potter to visit and–

The man appeared before the television as it flickered, the fellow precisely like the spectre of death from fairy tales with his giant scythe and black hood. Almost a cliché, really.

Reed jumped. "Shit."

Potter ignored his reaction, letting his robes settle as he lifted the scythe, the tool resting in both hands. "Mother sent me here to make good on one of your ill-advised promises. Follow me now."

Reed gulped down his drink then stood. "Lily Stephens?"

The reaper nodded, then swung his scythe at the still blinking television. Only a grey tear appeared, of course, and the man stepped within. Reed hopped after him with a grunt at the weight and heat of the Fringe – he'd been given no time to prepare of course, but at least Potter moved quickly through the crumbling rooms to another tear, this one leading to a short, gleaming corridor of black – as though tightly-packed coal rested behind glass.

Each footfall brought forth a sharp echo as they walked.

Here, in Aunty's mansion, the dangers of the Fringe receded but without Potter's protection, Reed knew he'd not last very long at all. Or at least, his human side wouldn't. The place wasn't quite the Underworld but it was more like her sprawling laboratory – only in an odd mix of industrial gothic mansion and strange hothouse.

Not that he'd seen *those* rooms very often.

Thankfully.

Instead, Potter led Reed through another door, then outside to a long stair – affording him a stretching view of the yard, its waving grass a pale white, with faint traces of luminous blue. The lawns were ringed here by paperbark trees, empty of leaves but the bark peeling like withering skin. Beyond them in turn, dark stone walls bursting up to the iron-grey of the sky.

But now, as they neared the ground and the edge of the building, the Waterwheel finally appeared.

Potter did not slow as he strode onward, but Reed did.

After all, how many times have you even seen that thing? Three? Four times maybe?

And the word 'waterwheel' was a little misleading since it suggested the singular... but the machine was a massive series of connected wheels feeding into other sizes, running at varying speeds and made of everything from bone to steel to wood to stone – even two of them made from glass that had been coloured in 'oil-spill-rainbow' and was somehow quite beautiful. There was even a wheel made of rubber, the material fascinating to Aunty.

The 'water' was another misnomer, since what powered the wheels where the machine sat within its mountain pool was in fact a stream of souls. They appeared as nothing more graceful than dark sludge; though hands, feet and faces occasionally pressed against the bounds of the liquid.

But there was no escape; some went back into the pool below, others straight out across the glass wheel to take another spin on the greater wheel of life, while others still were fed into... other places, to which he could not sense and had not received a clear answer when he asked.

Potter stopped before the wheels. "Very well, it is time to choose."

"Choose what?" Reed asked.

"Mother has granted your foolish promise under two conditions. You must decide whether you will accept them. If not, Lily Stephens will be returned at her scheduled time with an unmodified Fate Index."

Which would hardly guarantee that she'd get musical ability. Reed frowned at his cousin. "So, if I accept, her Index will be Curated?"

"Yes."

"All right. What do I have to do?"

"Make a decision upon hearing the conditions. First, she will be given a reduced lifespan."

Reed opened his mouth to object... but stopped. He was lucky he was getting *anything* and perhaps the second condition wouldn't be so bad? "How much shorter?"

"That is not knowledge for you or I."

"Fair enough."

"Second, she will be placed into the body of a Husk."

"Do you really have to call them that?" Reed said with a sigh.

"It is the proper term."

Reed shook his head. It wasn't, at all; but then, it was no use arguing with the man. And while it was a cruel word it was partially accurate – some poor woman had obviously lost all brain function and now lived in a vegetative state, her soul long-since harvested by one of Death's children. "Where?"

"A hospital in Melbourne, actually. You will be required to help Lily Stephens rebuild a life, however long it may or may not last."

"I accept," Reed said.

Potter raised a finger. "There is more. If you continue, you must be aware that you will be causing significant pain for her parents, and the one known as Lily too, since she will wake in the life of a different person, unable to act or recall in accordance with what the woman's parents once knew. More, Lily will be alone, a stranger in the life she occupies, surrounded by a host of people, objects and places that are empty of meaning to her."

Reed now found himself without words – and not by choice.

"You should abandon your promise, Reed."

"Give me a minute." He turned from the wheel, staring at the sick-looking trees and the mighty wall. What by all the Gods was the right choice? He'd promised her – and he couldn't break that promise... but at what cost?

How much suffering would he cause if he went through with it? *Shit.*

Did he really have the authority – and audacity – to

make the lives of others worse, just to give Lily a chance at a particular future?

And yet... Lily had helped him, risked herself twice.

Without her, he might not have been able to put a stop to Treveyos. *If you honour her request now, then you have to make sure things work out for her.*

No mistakes, either – it'll be your responsibility.

"Do it," Reed said as he turned back to the frowning man.

Chapter 5.

Reed paced his apartment, the coldness of Potter's disapproval still lingering in the dim room – obviously it had stayed since last night, when the man escorted him home without a word. *Maybe he actually* meant *to leave behind his displeasure, like an annoying omen of judgement.*

In two days Lily would be placed into the 'husk' at precisely midnight.

Reed had to be present, but until then he had enough to keep him distracted from the doubt that rattled around in his mind.

First, he had to pick up a little something from a disgruntled former casino employee. Finding one who'd worked there had not been difficult. And the price wasn't too bad either – at least, not now that Aunty's minions had made another payment. Ostensibly, it was something for all his work with the Shining Leaves, yet part of him knew there was a certain amount of charity involved. *Not that I didn't earn every damn cent.*

Many years ago he'd found himself offering an extended tutorial to Aunty about the realities of being human and needing money for nearly everything society offered. And she should have known – truly, she *did* know. Doubtless, not considering a concept like money as important or valid meant that Mors found it remarkably easy to overlook it.

In a way it was insulting... or maybe it could have hurt his pride, yet he'd never figured out a way to be insulted enough to turn down any offers. Her occasional acknowledgement that he had to deal with the reality of money was the only thing keeping him afloat sometimes.

Once Reed was downstairs and then inside his waiting taxi, it was a typically frustrating trip to the nearest shopping centre – sometimes a crawl, sometimes tearing down the roads at 60kms, but finally he paid his driver and stepped into the graceless building. It was little more than a series of rectangles plopped down in the middle of acres of parking, cars like frozen ants worshipping the mound.

Hopefully, his car would be salvageable without breaking the bank, but the RACV hadn't been too confident when he'd called.

Inside the shopping centre, the press of people and riot of gleaming brand names and exclamatory promotions washed over him as he angled toward a donut shop – Sprinkles. He got a fresh cinnamon donut and sat on the plastic chair to wait for 'Ben' who was dropping off the uniform.

Reed had finished his snack when a young fellow in a bright fast food uniform approached, large plastic bag in hand. He stopped at the table. "Cool coat. You Reed?"

He nodded. "Thanks."

Ben sat as he slid the bag over, but he kept his hand on it. "Look, before I give you this I should warn you. They can be pretty rough, you know?"

"Me too – but thanks again." Reed slid an envelope across the tiny square table. "You sure about this?"

The young man shrugged as he stood. "I mean, yeah. I was supposed to return it but once I moved, they gave up sending letters and once I blocked their account, e-mails too."

"Any one in particular I should look out for?"

"Yeah." Ben frowned. "Stupid prick called Alan. He's a fucking nut."

"Right."

"Well, see ya," the young man said as he walked away.

Reed opened the bag. Within, dark pants and the edge of a polo shirt with the casino's golden logo. Maybe he could have faked the cleaner's uniform instead, but the expired key card in the bag was probably just as useful as the clothing.

Or at least, I hope it will be.

Reed's next ride was shorter, to the station where he jumped upon a train and luckily found an empty carriage. He sat against a window where he tapped his foot. The sliding doors between carriages opened to reveal Max, his sunglasses concealing his eyes as he sauntered to the seat opposite and slumped down.

"Any news?"

Reed nodded. "I'm impressed; you didn't just snap into existence this time."

"I don't want to become predictable, you see." He folded one ankle across his knee. "Well?"

"See what you think of this," Reed said, as he explained what Emma had found, including the quote. "So we've got a film or a Stephen King buff – or, more likely, it's something older. The proverb dates from 1659, I think."

"Doubtless it's older again. After all, it gave old man Jupiter pause, right?"

"Should you really call him that?"

"Would you prefer 'Old man Zeus' then? Doesn't have the same ring to my ear."

"No, that's not what I meant, as I'm sure you're aware," Reed said with a grin. "But it's a good point. So, are you sending word back to him? Maybe he can help?"

"Mother will handle that once I report in." He shrugged. "Who knows, she might have spoken to Minerva already."

"So, was there something else?"

"Yes. You're going to be in a train accident."

Reed blinked.

"Quite soon, actually."

Reed shot to his feet. "What?"

Max rose and gripped him by the shoulders. "Don't worry. I'll take care of it."

"Max, what does that–"

Metal screamed.

The carriage flipped, colours streaking. The sound and snow of shattered glass was lost in the cacophony – his body had taken flight. Yet Max held him, his troubled gaze the only constant in the chaos. His eyes were endless tunnels that spanned eons, a sense of falling into them eliciting a shiver.

And then stillness.

Max released him.

They stood within a shattered carriage now, light and cold air streaming in from the torn roof. Something dripped, almost lost beneath creaking of heavy steel, of hissing from somewhere nearby. The doors to exit were twisted to an odd angle, and the next carriage was tilted. Beyond that no doubt things were worse.

"I'll be back," Max said, and blinked away; no doubt to begin duties as Reaper.

Oh God, how many?

Reed clambered over a carpet of glass and window frames, a fallen handrail giving him pause. But once he reached the next carriage he wrenched the sliding door open enough to squeeze into the twisted carriage. "Hello?" he called. "Does anyone need help?"

At the far end of the carriage, people were stumbling free, one person climbing from a shattered window.

Reed gripped the head rests as he moved between the aisles, glancing down as he did – until he found a small shape crumpled against the wall, which was now half 'floor' thanks to the crash.

A young girl, her dark hair covering her face, matted with blood.

His heart skipped a beat.

"Hey!" he called.

No answer. Reed climbed closer and reached down to lift the girl free, a sparkling Twix wrapper fell from her hand and she groaned. He exhaled. *Thank the gods.* "I'm taking you to your parents, okay?"

She did not answer clearly, but he stroked her head then started back toward his own carriage... then stopped. He wouldn't be able to pass through the doors with the girl. "Is anyone out there?" he called. "I've got a little girl."

A moment passed.

"Can anyone help us in here?" Reed shouted.

"Where are you?" a voice shouted back.

"Coming to the window."

Reed pulled himself up the sloped floor and moved down to the broken window – it had popped free from the frame and was now on the weed-strewn ground below, where a couple of people waited. Blood ran down from a cut on one woman's face, and a man was limping up to join them.

In the distance, the sound of sirens cried out.

"Can you take her?" Reed asked.

"I can."

Reed braced his legs with the seats then stretched down, handing the girl to the woman. Once she had the girl Reed sighed, smiling down at the strangers.

***

On the tracks of the rail line, surrounded by graffiti-covered fences, Reed stood back with his hands in the pockets of his coat. His throat grew tight as he watched more of his cousins moving through the line of wreckage. They moved to each crumpled figure and paused to speak gentle or calm words then blinked out of sight. Faint spirits followed them – human-like forms shaped from what had always looked like flower petals to Reed.

"How many?" he asked.

"Forty one," Potter replied. Max and Lina stood nearby, Valen too, his golden face downcast as he watched. Yet other cousins had gathered too – Mae, the happy woman Reed hadn't seen for years, and even little Conrad, who had his 'Oliver Twist' outfit on. It added to the 'cute' look of him – yet he was near as old as Potter. And like Mae, he didn't spend a lot of time in the city, mostly working interstate.

It should have been at least nice to see them again, to see so many of his extended family gathered in one place, but a sick anger had been building within him. Setting his fists to shaking where he hid them within his clothing.

"And it's my fucking fault."

"Unlikely," Potter replied. "You might have been a target but whoever derailed the train is clearly responsible. Consider it logically."

"Fuck logic."

Potter sighed.

"He's right, you know," Lina said. "And we'll figure this out. Whatever came up from underground wasn't necessarily after you."

"Maybe. But it'll be too late for everyone here – they all had plans. Something they were looking forward to. Tonight or tomorrow or next year, whatever. That's all gone now and if I'd been somewhere else today none of this..." he broke off and started walking down the tracks.

The emergency services were already moving through the crash site and it was best if he wasn't seen.

He'd not reached the still-distant station and its likely press of gawking morons when Conrad snapped into view before him. Reed side-stepped the child and continued on without a word. When he *did* reach the station he climbed onto the platform and pushed his way through the crowd and found a taxi rank, where he waited, tapping his foot, arms folded against the cold air.

Conrad reappeared but said nothing.

His cousin remained silent on the ride back home too, and Reed didn't start any conversation, since not only did it seem best to let the taxi driver keep thinking he was sane, but whatever Conrad had in mind could wait.

It's Devin that I actually need to speak to. I need to know more about the accident, more about whatever is down there.

And if not the werewolf, then perhaps one of Pluto's grubs?

Someone had to have seen something in the underground, to have *some* idea of exactly what was stalking him. Since it now seemed obvious that the timing of Devin's escape from the earth had not been an accident... had the wolf been *forced* to a point where Reed would be driving?

"That'll be $52, mate," the driver said.

Reed frowned as he reached into his wallet.

"Sorry, buddy. I'm not trying to rip you off."

"Nah, I believe you, just took me by surprise. And it's a shitload better than walking," he said as he handed over the money and exited the car.

He paused before his building, glancing down at Conrad. "I thought you might like to get inside first," said the child who was not a child at all, with a raised eyebrow.

"Right." Reed pulled open the door, stalked inside and smacked the button for the elevator. The doors slid shut, far too slowly, and they rode up in silence. It wasn't until he'd got inside his apartment, dumped his wallet and keys onto the bench, tossed his coat into the laundry and ramped up the heater that he spoke.

He pointed at the child waiting patiently by the door. "I don't want your opinion, you know."

Chapter 6.

Conrad sniffed. "Luckily, I'm not offering one."

"What is it then?" Reed said as he slumped into his armchair and lifted the remote, only to toss it onto the couch cushions. He didn't bother turning his head. "An order?"

"Not precisely. More like a clue."

"What?"

The kid appeared, perched upon the television now, legs dangling before the screen. "You want to alleviate some misplaced guilt – so find a grub and ask what's going on, maybe you'll get some answers."

"I've thought of that."

"I'd be disappointed if you hadn't," the boy said.

"So, your clue is something else?"

"Something related." Conrad hopped down and stood before Reed, a scythe snapping into his grip. He tilted the blade so that the mirror-like surface now faced Reed. "Look."

Something large and dark sprawled across a green field, spots of red clear despite the thing being shadowed by grandstands... it was the MCG, though no cricket or football games were currently being played. At least, not until tomorrow night. And yet, the spirit-worm appeared to be feasting happily enough.

Reed glanced back to Conrad. "Are you telling me you think the spirit-worm is responsible?"

"No, Reed. But I think you should check anyway because that's near to the size of the last one you found. Maybe it has something to do with your parents?"

Reed glanced to the kitchen where the knucklebone rested within a small box, still upon the kitchen table. *Is it possible?*

Conrad snapped his fingers and the scythe disappeared. "In any event, I think I'll get back to work."

"Thanks," Reed said.

The boy laughed – and it was somewhere between a giggle and a chuckle – a fairly disturbing sound to be honest. "*Now* you remember your manners."

He disappeared before Reed could reply.

The kid had a point... Reed pushed himself up and out of the chair. Something else *had* to happen first. He'd put Elise off once more. He muttered a curse; setting her case aside was becoming tediously predictable and yet he was doing it again.

Maybe a train crash is a fair reason.

But what had been fair about her fate? The spirit-worm would have to wait a little longer perhaps – it was time to place some pretty fucking huge bets.

He strode into the kitchen and started gathering the necessary bits and pieces for a cheese and vegemite sandwich – like a kid – then pacing as he chewed. It was time to try his luck at the casino. Some sort of answer waited there and it was past time to collect.

Once finished, Reed jumped into the shower. He let the hot water sear his shoulders as he closed his eyes, letting the steam fill the room. Unbidden, the sound of screeching steel returned. He shuddered. *I got lucky but a lot of people didn't. Whoever did derailed that train has a lot to answer for.*

When his skin of his fingers had turned prune-like, Reed cut the water and stepped out to dry off and change into the casino uniform, polo and black slacks, locking up and riding the elevator back down; this time sharing the ride with a pair of teenage girls who giggled over their mobile phones.

And then it was a tram toward the city centre – no train this time – and finally, he found himself standing on the footpath before the towering casino, twenty-something floors of fancy rooms, too many of them home to the gleaming misery of gambling, cocktails and drugs.

He shivered at the cold; should have brought his coat along.

Inside, somewhere, was his answer.

And I'm going to tear the place apart to find it if I have to.

Reed strode through the glass doors, hit by a blast of warm air, shoes clapping on the polished stone floors. The chatter of a large water-feature partially masked the awfully-bright music from pokie machines, water almost glowing beneath a golden light display.

He headed for the nearest information desk with what he hoped was a somewhat sheepish smile. "Hi, I'm starting here today but I'm having a bit of trouble," he told the woman on the desk.

"I'll try help," she replied, setting a pen and paper aside. She'd already noted the logo upon his polo and smiled.

"I'm supposed to be cleaning... ah, upstairs I think, but they sent me the wrong uniform. And on my way I dropped my keycard – it fell down the storm water drain. Caught a glimpse of the three chips and then it was just gone."

She chuckled. "Poor guy. Look, take this one and go visit Jacinta in maintenance, she'll get you set up. It's basement one."

"Thanks heaps," Reed said as he accepted the 'replacement' card.

He set off for the shiny elevator doors and pressed the button then tapped his foot as he waited. When the doors finally dinged, he let a suit and its arm candy exit, then slipped inside. He did not glance back to the information desk; no need to draw attention by giving off such an obvious sign of guilt. *Hopefully she's too busy to look over here and see that I'm not going down at all.*

Once the doors closed he grunted. *Time to test this thing.* He waved the card before the panel above a glowing column of buttons, then hit the Penthouse.

The elevator began an upward glide. "Thank the gods."

It was an almost soundless passage. *Fancy building, fancy lift.* Despite the smoothness, he folded his arms with a frown. Somehow, the glitz was more annoying than it ought to have been – the anger that fuelled him returning now that he didn't have to fake anything.

But if he could find another cleaner to probe for dirt on Dunstall then he'd have to clamp down on it again – either that, or use it. And truly, some poor sap just doing their job didn't deserve to be roughed up.

When the doors opened once more, it was to a hallway

lined with prints of sleek modern art in thin, golden frames. There were even sideboards with crystal vases and fresh flowers – real or fake, it looked nice enough. His first step actually sank into the plush carpet. But he started down the corridor toward a pair of closed double doors, however, there was no manner of upmarket 'do not disturb' notice.

He knocked once when he reached them. "Housekeeping."

No answer. Reed frowned as he inserted the key card into the door. A green light flashed and then the door clicked open. The interior was similar enough to the hallways, though at least one wall had no reproductions; a television took up half the space and the lounge furniture facing it was all white leather. *To hell with cleaning those things when some rich prick spills a drink.*

Reed slowed his exploration before the en suite door – steam escaped in wisps; the sound of running water growing louder.

He shook his head. "Shit." Was there really any way to be wrong about what was behind the door? *Even with my rule about assumptions?* But there was another rule – or at least, something he liked to remember – nothing poetic, but it came to mind now. *The world believes in bad luck before good.*

Reed reached out and turned the handle, then pulled the door open.

Steam rushed free. Water splashed against the glass walls of a massive shower... and a figure slumped in the corner. Reed waved at the steam as he crept closer. A middle-aged man, naked, motionless. And judging from the grey pallor to his face, dead. And the guy was familiar... was it Jordan from SEDO?

"What the hell is going on here?" he whispered.

Had Dunstall been cleaning house? If so, that assumed there truly was a direct link between the druglord and Treveyos... which was looking increasingly likely. And precisely how had Jordan died? No sign of a broken neck or open wounds. Overdose?

Footsteps thundered from outside.

Reed spun.

Shouting followed as men burst into the suite, several in police uniform but one wearing the plain clothes of a detective. This man was leading with his gun. He was an older fellow but seemed spry as he gestured with the barrel. "Hands on your head."

Reed lifted his arms with a sigh.

Chapter 7.

Duong sat across from Reed in the sparse interrogation room, similar enough to the one at the man's own station; though a voice recorder and his phone sat between them to immortalise the interview, instead of a camera in the corner. The detective was smoking again, his sleeves rolled back and his cheeks unshaven as he waited for an answer. His clenched jaw moved slightly too, as if chewing on constrained fury.

Beside Duong sat the detective who'd burst in to Dunstall's penthouse. This fellow leant back in his chair, tie and suit immaculate and expression quite calm beneath silver hair.

Reed lifted his handcuffs onto the table with a clink. "I'm not lying so I can say the same thing again if you want. I was as shocked as you to find that guy in there. He was a lead for me, not a target."

Duong shook his head.

Detective McPherson rubbed his chin. "It always comes back to this for me, Mr Lavender. You were impersonating an employee and you'd broken into that room where we found you with the deceased; a man whose company had previously filed a harassment complaint against you."

"None of those things make me responsible for his death."

"None of them make you seem trustworthy, either, Reed," Duong snapped. "What the hell are you up to?"

McPherson raised a hand. "Want to finish that outside, Detective?"

"Yeah." Duong sucked in a long draw as he stood, opening and then closing the door a little firmly – not exactly slamming it, but close enough.

"You've worked with Duong a few times before, right?"

"Yeah."

"I guess he's frustrated; he probably thought he could trust you, you know?"

Reed frowned. "Do you want me to establish some sort of notion that I don't even think that I myself am a trustworthy person? Is that where you're trying to go with this?"

The man smiled. "I'm going where my nose leads me, which is to your history." He tapped a file. "And some of it is impressive. You've helped various police agencies solve a few serious crimes over the years; you're good at what you do. But there are things in here that are odd."

That was hardly a small list if they've done their research. "Such as?"

"Firstly, the disappearance of your parents. There is also a case with the apparent group suicide you appear to have stumbled across some years ago. Or a client that was struck down by heart failure in an abandoned property in Western Australia."

Reed frowned. "Now I'm being accused of being involved with whatever happened to my own parents?"

"I did not say that."

"Then what did you say, exactly?"

"That strange things have happened around you in the past. And now, this business with Petros Martin, Jordan Miller and SEDO. Something is obviously not right."

"I agree. And Robert Dunstall is responsible."

"So you claim," he said with a chuckle. "But it's not my job to just believe anything from a suspect's mouth – I'm sure you understand that."

"Well, we disagree about one thing. I'm not a suspect; I'm actually the culprit."

The man frowned.

"You've got me on breaking and entering. I clearly did exactly that but we don't even know how or why Jordan died, so why am I still here talking about that? Isn't it time to charge me and show me to my cell?"

Detective McPherson folded his arms. "Don't try and shit-talk me, Mr Lavender. I know you're not a fucking clown so tell me, if our roles were reversed – would you let me wander off without questioning?"

Reed shrugged. "No."

"Fine. So, let's be honest."

"I am. I'm not saying that I'd let you walk away but I'd listen to your answers and follow up on them," Reed replied.

"They don't satisfy me. You've obviously got an axe to grind with these guys, and your theories about the link between SEDO and the girl's murder haven't panned out, right?"

"They led me to Dunstall, actually."

"But he wasn't in that room – you were."

Reed sighed. "Come on, Detective McPherson, you don't actually think I buy that, do you?"

He frowned. "Buy what, exactly?"

"That you believe a powerful druglord needs to be physically present in order to knock off someone he considers deadweight."

"So, now it's a hit?"

"Aren't we waiting on the autopsy for cause of death?"

Detective McPherson stood with a grin. "We are. So stick around until then, all right?"

Reed leant back in his own chair but didn't answer as the man headed for the door. As the older detective exited, he motioned for Duong to re-enter. And while Duong now carried no cigarette, he'd certainly managed to drag the stale scent of smoke in with him as he slumped into his chair.

"Welcome back."

Duong glared across the table. "Cut the crap, Reed."

"Cut me loose and I will."

"Fat chance," he replied. "But if you've got nothing else to say then sit there and shut up for a minute, will you?" Yet his eyes locked on to Reed's and he lifted a pen and notepad from his pocket and began writing.

He slid the notepad across the desk.

Something's going on here and I don't know how it's going to turn out for you.

Reed started to respond but caught himself. He raised an eyebrow.

Duong took the pad bad and wrote again. *I've been told to bury you with this.*

Reed leant closer as a chill spread across his body.

Again, Duong scribbled in his pad, the writing growing progressively more rushed. *They want me to make something stick with this case. Anything. Tried to ask why and got told to shut my mouth.*

He took the pad back and returned it to his pocket, and continued to sit in silence.

Reed could not stop frowning.

Gods, who wants a piece of me now?

Eventually, the door opened once more and Detective McPherson returned, two cups of coffee in hand. He offered one to Duong then looked to Reed. "So, one more time before we show you to a little cell downstairs."

"Is it a private cell at least?" Reed asked.

"You're in luck, actually." He snorted. "You need your beauty sleep or something, Mr Lavender?"

Reed laughed. "You've been saving that joke since your rookie year, right?"

Detective McPherson narrowed his eyes. "Listen, piss ant. You're not on top here – so start talking or I'll take you down there myself and you can cool off with a few new bruises, how does that sound?"

"Like you just offered up some police brutality on tape."

McPherson snatched up his drink and strode to the door. "Duong, take him."

"Right." Duong rose with a frown and started around the table, motioning for Reed to stand. "Hurry up, then."

Chapter 8.

Duong leant against the cell bars, face mostly shadowed in the sub-standard light. Reed sat on the end of his narrow bed, close enough to hear the Detective's low words. But he kept his head hung low, just in case the cameras were good enough to read lips... which seemed unlikely, considering the light.

Thanks a lot, paranoia.

But then, it was only paranoia if he was wrong and that seemed unlikely. Someone in the police had a plan to silence him one way or another. Maybe pushing McPherson had been a bit much. "You think Dunstall has someone among the higher ups then," Reed said.

The detective nodded. "Or at the least, he's got to have some serious leverage."

"So what do you think?"

"That you need to stay put until I can sort something out. I'm on a tightrope here, and you haven't made things any easier."

"Come on, you think it's a coincidence that the police

got a tip just in time to 'catch' me with Jordan Miller's body?"

"I don't know what to think, to be honest. Maybe the desk clerk didn't like the look of you?"

"I think she bought it."

"Or maybe you've been holding back for months and now it's come back to bite you in the arse. Maybe it's just your stupid obsession with the girl's case."

Reed looked up with a frown. "It's not stupid, Duong."

"You know what I mean. It's making you fuck things up, isn't it?"

"That's a matter of perspective – I'm closer than ever."

He pushed himself away from the bars. "That perspective meant to include a cell?"

"Nice one."

"Take this seriously, Reed. If it *is* a set-up then who out there knows your movements well enough to pull it off? You're probably being watched."

Reed frowned. That wasn't far-fetched. *Maybe I've let myself become too single-minded again.*

"Just keep your head down until I figure this out," he added as he started for the distant door. "And don't fuck this up for me, you're not the only one in danger."

"Right," Reed said.

He lay back on the bed with a sigh. Despite all the bravado, things *had* taken an explicitly poor turn. It wasn't just the setback in Elise's murder, nor being held in custody in connection with a possible homicide. Nor was it being prevented from investigating whoever had taken Feronia's hand, or the new Spirit-worm or whatever was happening underground, but he had a responsibility to turn up at the hospital for Lily too.

It's all getting a bit much.

"Shit."

"Trouble, cousin?"

The voice echoed from a nearby cell.

Reed rose as Max stepped through the wall with a smile. His cousin now wore a cartoonish prison jumpsuit complete with black and white stripes. He glanced at Reed. "I see prisons don't really coordinate as much as they used to," he said.

"What?"

"Your clothing."

Reed sighed. "Max, this is a holding cell, not a prison, as I'm sure you know."

"So, you're happy to see me then?" Max said with a grin.

"Yes."

"Good, then I'll break you out if you want to leave." He snapped his fingers and a large scythe appeared, blade gleaming as if with its own light.

"I do, but I don't know if I can."

"Why not? I'll protect you from the Fringe, you know that."

"No, it's because if I just disappear it'll put Duong in danger – I'm not sure how much, either. Something's going on here."

Max tossed the scythe over his shoulder and it disappeared. "Fine, I suppose I could arrange something."

"Like what?"

He grinned. "Just wait a little while and I'll be back. I've been wanting to use this for a long time now... I just hope it works."

"Max?"

"Trust me, I think I've thought of everything."

Reed stood. "Comforting. What about Aunty?"

"Meaning?"

"Isn't this against her new rules?"

He spread his hands. "She'll see the necessity of it, I'm sure."

"That makes one of us."

Max disappeared.

Reed slumped back onto the cot but it was no good, he had to pace until finally, he moved to the bars and peered out. The nearest other occupied cell was some distance away, a pair of hands visible where they rested upon the crossbar. *Something I should have checked before.* Not that he and Max had been yelling, but still, carelessness was rarely rewarded with good fortune.

"Ready?"

Reed turned.

Max stood in the cell once more, still wearing his ridiculous outfit, only now it included a miner's helmet with a light. Max had been joined by the stout humanoid form of a grub, the fellow waiting patiently. He could have been the same one from the first Spirit-worm or not, differences were difficult to discern. Like that first grub, his hands appeared to be cloaked in dark mittens but it was more the servant's dark skin.

"You're having fun, aren't you?" Reed asked Max.

"I'm glad you like the hat. So, I have something else but Lina is bringing it – while we wait, let me talk you through the plan."

"Mention the worm too, won't you?" the grub said.

"Indeed."

"I can guess half of it," Reed replied. "Pluto's servant here is going to take me down through the earth so I can escape, right?"

"Right. We could still use the Fringe, I suppose, but Pluto himself asked me to step up your investigation into the Spirit-worm; he lent me Rhubarb here to help out. That's why I'm a little late."

"Rhubarb?"

The grub shrugged. "It's an approximation of my name."

"Then, pleased to meet you. I'm Reed."

"I know that," he said with a nod. "But we're happy to have your help. This is the second large scale concentration in a short span. We need you to help us understand why this is happening and since you're mostly human maybe you'd know."

Reed had a brief, uncharitable thought – wasn't there anyone else who could help out? But he buried it. Maybe others *were* out there investigating too but he just didn't know about it. In any event, he was going to demand assistance from any and all. "I'll do my best. But what about Duong? I can't just disappear, remember?"

"That's what Lina's bringing – it's a doll," Max said.

"Meaning?"

Lina appeared; a blank, featureless marionette in her arms – approximately the size of a human. But it was not made from wood, steel or plastic, but some manner of white clay... at a guess. "I'll shape this to look like you," she said. "I just need some hair or a fingernail, Reed."

"Hair will do fine," he said, plucking a few from his head and handing them over.

"Perfect," she said. "I'll control the doll but it won't

be able to do much. I'm bending the rules here; we're not allowed to use surrogates of flesh. It's only clay."

"Max said he'd handle Aunty, luckily," Reed said with a grin.

"Only if you get results."

"Ah, asking for forgiveness does tend to be easier than permission."

"Exactly. Now, time for us to get underground," Max said.

Rhubarb took Reed's hand and knelt to place the other on the stone floor. Steam rose, but it caused no scent or real damage, and instead, a grey shimmering appeared beneath them.

Together, they started to sink into the floor. He glanced at Lina. "Don't make that 'me' do anything I wouldn't do myself."

She nodded as her hands moved in a blur, moulding the head toward what seemed to be his face. "Trust me; he'll be a model prisoner."

Darkness blocked his view then as he closed his eyes.

The sense of movement soon passed and ground solidified beneath his boots. Reed opened his eyes to a predictably dark storm water access tunnel of stone, but Max flicked his helmet's light on – and lit the walls with a blast worthy of deer lights. "Neat, huh?"

"Yes. I was afraid you were going to choose something inconspicuous."

"Nothing down here will bother us."

"Well, I'm not convinced of that, Max." He explained about the thing which had chased Devin out of the underground.

"Hmmm. Doesn't sound like a Spirit-worm at all."

"Then let's be watchful," Rhubarb said. Then, he stomped off along the passage. "But *while* we walk."

"Yes, sir," Max replied with a quick salute.

Reed groaned.

Chapter 9.

Yet no mysterious creatures attacked on their journey through the underground – a direct path which was usually achieved by having the grub take him through stone or dirt. Sometimes their path was up and sometimes down, but often simply *through* the graffiti-covered walls, other times splashing through thin trails of water that steamed when he used his hands.

When at last they reached the Spirit-worm, Reed slowed to a halt as Max offered a low whistle.

"Here we are, beneath one of the stadiums humans enjoy visiting," Rhubarb said.

The giant Spirit-worm filled the entire tunnel where it lay pulsing red and black beneath the bowels of the stadium. Or, more accurately perhaps, it lay beneath the stadium... and the tunnel just happened to be part of the space the worm had filled, since the thing spread through the walls and into very earth too.

Just like the previous worm, this one was covered in stout grubs that clambered across the dark surface. When they streamed by, often simply passing into the walls, their arms were filled with dark smudges of ephemeral... something.

"Well, there it is," the grub said.

"Yes."

He looked up. "Any ideas?"

"Well..." Reed exhaled. He didn't have much at all. Though maybe it was obvious... maybe. "They form around negative emotions, right?"

"As you know."

"And there's a sporting stadium above."

Rhubarb made a snuffling sound that may or may not have been a sound to indicate impatience. "Meaning?"

Max clicked his light off as he answered. "That humans tend to release some of their ugliest emotions at these places."

"And afterwards," Reed added. "There's honour and sportsmanship here too, but it's not always so noble."

"Ah. Nothing new to us," the grub said with a wave of his mitten-like hand. "Perhaps a little more context is needed. Before, I mentioned that two worms of such a size appearing in such a short time remained somewhat unprecedented, yes?"

"You did."

"Well, for further context we would say that something one twentieth of the size of this one typical for a sporting event, and this worm has built up swiftly over the last few days – *after* the last event above I'll add, not during."

Max was frowning now. "And there's nothing up there, not even training right now."

Reed exhaled. Troubling indeed, but it was a mystery he was ill-quipped to solve, surely? If Spirit-worms were based on numbers of negative emotions and few people were above, then did that mean something *inhuman* resided within the stadium? "Max, do you feel anything evil up there? I certainly can't."

"What kind of evil?"

"The non-human kind."

"No." He shook his head. "Nothing like that, unless they're hiding *very* well."

"Then, could a single human be bad enough to generate such a Spirit-worm?"

"I doubt Hilter or Pol Pot are strolling around up there."

"Then doesn't that suggest this *isn't* a human problem at all?"

The grub pointed to the worm. "They are born of human emotions, half-skull."

"Right." He frowned at the dirty concrete beneath his feet. *So if there's nothing above and it's always human-driven...* "What about below?"

Rhubarb glanced down with a slow nod. "Hmmm There doesn't *seem* to be anything below the Spirit-worm but we'll check. It's not usually something we focus on, since the humans tend to be above ground when they excrete," the grub said with a shrug.

"Excrete?"

"That's the technical term, yes."

"Then let me know what you find," Reed said. "I'll help if you need me again but I've got somewhere I need to be."

Max switched off his light. "I'll have someone take you, assuming it's in the city."

"Thanks," Reed said. "It's a hospital, actually."

Rhubarb had already charged off toward the spirit-worm

and one of his fellows.

"So, what about the doll?" Max asked.

"Let's leave it in place until I need to get out of there properly."

"I'll ask Lina to keep an ear out then."

"Right. Once I take care of Lily, I've got just one more thing to do. After that I want to check in with Emma again. Maybe she'll have found something else."

"Let's hope so – the rest of us are still a little stumped."

"No clues at all?"

"Nothing I'd bet on," Max replied with a shrug. "Just the same guesses and hesitation, really."

"So, you think Aunty and the other Gods are dragging their feet too?"

He nodded. "For several reasons. The Rules, of course. Once someone breaks them everyone else might, and for less justifiable reasons. I *also* think that some of them are afraid."

"Of whoever took Feronia's hand?"

"Yes. Because they cannot find the truth, and that suggests that someone out there is just so damn good at hiding themselves."

Reed nodded. "That makes sense, at least."

"I think so too, but to be honest, half of them secretly suspect the other half of being behind this, which is maybe a little irrational, because Jupiter himself cannot find a straight answer." He sighed. "I know we like to lay it on thick when it comes to mocking humans for being childish but to be honest, we're not that much better, sometimes."

"Wow, that's something I never thought I'd hear, Max."

He chuckled. "But if anyone was going to say it, you

knew it would be me, right?"

Reed joined his laughter. "I suppose so."

Chapter 10.

The hospital lay in a darkened hush, almost haunted by the beep of medical equipment. Normally white walls were a dull grey and the midnight moon snuck in between open curtains, enough to let light fall upon a Monet print, full of shadows where it rested above the bed.

The glow of the life-support machine kept him company in the chair where he sat beside the poor woman. Whoever it was, he could not say – despite his extremely official-looking doctor's disguise, he hadn't tried to get his hands on her chart or any other paperwork.

Better not to know – maybe it'll ease the guilt.

There was some excitement for Lily in him somewhere, but the dark-haired woman lying in the bed before him had a family who'd soon be overjoyed... followed by the creeping realisation that something was *very* different. He stood, jaw clenched. "Shit."

Was this a mistake after all?

The woman was perhaps nearly thirty and her hair was dark and short. She still had some freckles on her cheeks and her nose seemed sharper than Lily's... they weren't too similar. *How will Lily handle that?*

The machine's beeping changed and Reed turned.

Her eyes fluttered and she flinched. Reed leant a little closer. The woman shot straight up, blinking hard. He fell back with a gasp, his heart thumping.

She turned to frown at him. "Reed?"

"Hello, Lily," he replied, keeping his voice soft.

The woman – who was now Lily – shivered as she ran one hand down her forearm to squeeze her own fingers. "Oh my god, it worked." She patted her own cheek, then swallowed. "I'm different."

"Did Potter explain?"

"Yeah. Stupid thing to say, I guess... it's just, I didn't think it would *feel* so different."

"You are older, I guess."

She nodded, looking around the dim room as she did. "Everything looks so solid, even in the dark. Like it'd be really heavy."

"Being alive is a lot of work, I suppose," he said as he leant forward once more. "This might be harder than you thought, Lily."

"Her family?"

He nodded. "Your family too, now. You have more than one."

Her face brightened a little. "But my real family is still alive too, right?"

"I think so. But I don't think you should be trying to visit them right away. Maybe not for a long time." He sighed. "Or at all, I don't know."

Her smile faded. "Potter explained that too."

"Well, you have me in the meantime," he said. He handed her a business card. "You can call me any time if you get freaked out."

"Thanks. You really came through, you know."

"I hope that's true. There's a cost to keeping your memories and I just hope it's not too high."

"I'm glad I don't know."

"I understand."

"So, other things might be a little different compared to when you were here last," he said, and started through a few of them. Mostly around technology and entertainment, but she remained interested for a while. However, her eyes soon began to droop and he apologised. "You're probably tired."

"I guess I am. I didn't know how hard it would be to return... my limbs don't feel very strong."

"It'll get easier each day." He stood, glancing at the darkness beyond the window. His entire body seemed to be made of stone itself; a weariness that dragged at him, right down to his eyelids. "I'm sorry to leave you so soon but I think I should rest too. I've a couple of things to do. It's not much of an excuse, I know."

"Is it about Elise?"

"Yeah."

"Good luck," she said. "And I will text, you know, Reed. Be ready."

"I will," he said as he smiled, and started for the doorway. He paused before leaving. "One more tip; I think you should find a mirror while you're alone. It'll probably be unpleasant – you won't see what you imagine yourself to look like."

A slight frown crossed her brow, and fear flashed across her eyes but she shrugged, a weak gesture. "Thanks. You're probably right. But I won't complain; that wouldn't be fair to Jane's body."

"Is that her name?"

Lily looked down at her hands. "Yeah."

"Well, you know she's not using it, and she's better off waiting for her next turn than stuck here."

"Yeah."

"Good luck," Reed said as she settled back into the pillows and closed her eyes.

He started down the hall at a stride. His boots clapped on the linoleum, echoing in the quiet. He passed darkened nurse stations and waiting rooms of glass and brighter colours, but before reaching a more populated part of the hospital, he slowed to lean against a wall, breathing hard all of a sudden.

Shit.

He glanced back toward Lily's room. *What if this is the wrong thing to do? She seemed okay but how long will that last?*

Yet breaking a promise wasn't right either.

"Damn it."

Reed pushed himself from the wall and started toward the light and eventually, the exit. He had plenty of time to reach the morgue but somehow, the sooner he got outside the further he'd leave his doubt behind.

Chapter 11.

"Good morning. I'm Dr Desio and I need to see the body of…" Reed paused in the flat, bluish light of the city morgue, pulling a notepad from one of his coat pockets as he did, "Jordan Miller, please."

The young man on the front desk frowned as he clicked at his computer. He was still blinking and a take-away cup of morning coffee steamed nearby. "Oh, is there something wrong? I didn't know the Royal was sending anyone over first thing."

He smiled. "Just routine, really. Won't take more than a few minutes."

"Okay. If you'd like to wait, I could get Dr Rosen to show you in."

Reed hesitated. Finding where Jordan's body had been kept and then gaining access to the morgue had taken enough trouble, best not to risk too many more face-to-face interactions where he could trip up. "I actually have another appointment I'm needed for; I'm just stopping in on my way. If Dr Rosen isn't around, I'm sure I'll be fine you if show me in."

"I suppose so. Just a minute." The young man rose and led Reed to a sterile, steel-looking theatre where the fellow flicked on the lights. The air was thick with... chemicals and other unpleasant things. A few bodies lay upon tables, covered by white sheets. Sharp and serious-looking surgical gear rested on stainless steel trolleys, and a box of blue rubber gloves.

"Sorry," the assistant said as he pored over some paperwork. "Mr Miller is here somewhere is in... number twelve."

"Thanks." Reed went to the wall of silver 'hole in the wall' style chambers and pulled on the handle. The corpse slid out upon the rail, not as heavy as it ought to have been, perhaps due to the bearings on the slider. Reed pulled back the sheet to reveal a grey face.

"Here you are, Dr Desio," the assistant said, handing over a manila folder.

Reed opened it and nodded, as though he understood exactly what he was looking at. "Thanks again, won't be long."

"Right." The man excused himself.

Reed skimmed the information in the file. Cause of death had been overdose on diamorphine, no surprise there. But there was a blow to the head. It could have been sustained by falling in the shower. Other minor bruising was mentioned, but all post-mortem. No next of kin was listed anywhere... though hopefully that wouldn't be necessary. There was still the other SEDO worker, Tracy, to hunt down, if needed.

Reed hovered a hand over the man's neck, then let his consciousness seep down into the victim. "In the name of Mors, speak any that you might," he whispered. And though he meant the next words to some extent, they were not so heartfelt as when he'd called upon Elise. Still, his conviction didn't matter – all who could answer did, no exceptions. "I'll help you if you can."

A rasping whisper followed. "How's the new guy working out?"

Reed hung his head.

Useless.

He covered the body and shoved the tray back into the locker. It thumped a little hard, but he pushed his frustration down as he headed for the door. *There's still one more person worth visiting.*

Outside, he thanked the assistant as he left, then started down the street. It was a row of shiny sedans and parking meters as his feet slapped upon the damp footpath. Up ahead, the traffic converged toward a tram stop, it's brightly coloured timetable like a beacon.

Once there, he joined the other folks in coats and umbrellas, closing his eyes a moment as he exhaled. It'd been a long couple of days. *Incisive understatement there, Reed.*

Tracy from SEDO.

Were the offices still open? Or had the cult fallen apart since Treveyos' death? *I should have kept an eye on that myself.* Either way, he'd have to find what Tracy knew... he opened his eyes.

Tracy was probably a mistake.

SEDO was a distraction.

He set off at a run, heading for a still-distant taxi rank. He swore beneath his breath as he dodged dog-walkers and the elderly – but the frustration was directed his own way... somehow, he'd fallen into an assumption. A big mistake – the worst mistake too, his first damn rule.

It wasn't necessarily true that Elise had been killed because she rejected Treveyos' cult. *Maybe* she'd been initiated into the fold and seen too much. *Maybe* she tried to get away because she saw something supernatural at SEDO, something that understandably would have freaked her out...

And maybe not.

"You're an idiot."

Seeing SEDO online convinced her to head for the city; that much was *likely* at the least. But the assumption SEDO caused her to run had become a premise for his recent attempts to find answers. And perhaps a faulty one at that.

It was just as likely that she ran after being forced into drug trafficking – and he'd considered that notion before, early on. *But I shouldn't have neglected that possibility.*

He needed a different path to Dunstall. Not SEDO, but Froud at the nightclub. If Elise rejected a role as dealer or mule then wasn't *Froud* the path to Dunstall? The casino tip might have actually been two things – one, a fact about Dunstall's behaviour and two, a way to get Reed out of the car.

Which meant a return visit was in order.

Only this time, he'd do it with some muscle.

Chapter 12.

Reed approached the Outer Limits gym, his wallet considerably lighter now, where it took up the corner of the block, pausing beneath its silver and black sign. The O lived within the howl of a wolf. *Hardly subtle, Devin.*

He reached for the door but stepped back when someone exited; a woman who smiled at him as she passed. Yet a man in a black shirt with the gym's logo ran after her, calling as he did, phone in hand.

"Miss? Is this your phone?"

She turned. "Oh, yes! Thank you."

He handed it over and returned, glancing to Reed as he did. "Morning."

Paradoxically, the fellow's plain face was familiar… from the club? The customer who was a little more than human! "I think we've met before," Reed said, extending a hand.

The werewolf blinked, but smiled. "Oh, the Reaper from the Old Royal. Are you here to see Devin?"

"I am actually."

"He's due back any minute I think, but Grace is in the office."

"I can ask her my question too, if you think she's not too busy." In her were-form Grace had silvery fur, making her a striking match beside Devin. She was a woman of few words but would still help. Probably.

"Sure, I'll show you to the office," the fellow said, pushing in to the gym.

Brittle dance music thumped away in the background, nothing too loud, since most of the people working out upon the gleaming machines had headphones or air pods. A couple laughed together as they jogged the treadmill and Reed had to give them credit. If he had to run on a mill he'd not have the breath for laughter, that's for sure.

"I thought you were just passing through...?" Reed asked.

The man held out a hand. "Patrick. Yeah, I was but Devin offered me a place if I wanted it."

"Nice."

His guide stopped at the open door to an office set off behind a sleek counter.

"Grace? You have a visitor," he said.

Grace looked up from a laptop, her slim figure and pale hair seeming to suggest some fragility – though that was a mistake to believe so. He'd once seen her and Devin take down a Highway Troll together, tearing it half to pieces in order to protect a cub. The blood spray had crossed the freeway.

"Reed? This is a surprise." She nodded to Patrick, who returned to the desk with a smile.

"Hello, Grace," Reed replied. "I was hoping to ask you and Devin for a favour."

She gestured to a chair across from her own.

He sat and glanced over his shoulder to the open door

and the gym members, before lowering his voice. "Devin told you about the underground?"

Grace nodded, a hint of concern in her gaze now.

"Well, I've got some friends working on that but I wanted to ask about something else. Any of your family looking to let off some steam?"

"How so?"

"I want to put some pressure on a dealer – I need to confirm a hit, then deliver some justice."

"Do you mean vengeance?" She leant back in the chair, expression difficult to read.

"Actually, I'm not sure yet. I might be out of leads, if this doesn't pan out."

"You asking for fang or fist?"

"Maybe fang."

She exhaled. "I don't know. Maybe ask Patrick – he's new enough not to know any better."

"Thanks," Reed said as he stood. "I'm in your debt again."

"You are."

He thanked her but had only taken a single step when she stopped him, using his name softly, the sound of doubt still clear. "Reed?"

"Yes?"

"Why aren't you getting your cousins to help you with this?"

"Aunty is cracking down on that sort of thing."

"This have something to do with that business from a little while ago?"

"It's connected, yeah. I'm going to get to the bottom of it though," he said, the words more confident than they ought to have been.

"Right. Well, tell Patrick he has my blessing if he agrees."

"Will do," he replied. "Any ideas on what I'll owe, exactly? I only ask because last time I ended up spending far more time in the –"

Grace raised a hand. "Devin will be in touch when we need you, Reed."

He sighed as he left.

***

Luckily, Patrick was indeed interested in blowing off some steam.

"It's a lot more satisfying than just working out, you know," the werewolf said from the passenger seat of Reed's new rental car, the glow from a streetlight illuminating half of his face. His shadowed eye glowed golden. "Especially when we can't go on a really good run."

"Well, this might not be that simple, you know," Reed said. "There's a risk here."

Patrick raised an eyebrow. "Only if they're packing silver."

"Well, *I* can die, you know."

"Can you? I thought you Reapers were immortal?"

Reed rocked a hand back and forth. "I'm half human so that complicates things."

"Yeah, but can't you just, I dunno... come back if you die?"

"Depends on a few things but I think we should go over this once more."

"No probs."

"Right. We go in – but this time I want to surprise Froud inside. Once he heads in the back, we're following, even if we have to kick the door down," Reed said. "And by we, I mean you, of course."

"Can do."

"Good. We deal with whoever he's got inside, then I need you to barricade whatever interior door, right?"

"No problems there, either."

"Then, if I can't convince him to give up the name, you can try – let him see the change, if you're still okay with that."

"I'm not ashamed," Patrick said with a nod. "What if he doesn't talk?"

Reed scratched at the stubble on his cheek. "That's the part I haven't figured out."

"Your call, I guess."

"Thanks," Reed said with a chuckle. "The thing is, this guy *did* give me a number and I think it was the one he uses for his hit-man. And it feels like it wasn't fake – I gave Froud the scare of his life when we last talked. But whoever owns the mailbox never called me back – probably checked me out, instead."

"Your own phone, was it?"

"Yeah. Clumsy of me but I had other things on my mind at the time."

"So you're worried that this Froud won't actually know how to get in contact with the trigger-man?"

"Yes. There are things we can do to him... but if he truly doesn't know then we're wasting our time."

Patrick tapped the dashboard. "But you still have to go in and rule him out one way or another, right?"

"I do."

"Then let's go. I'm ready."

Reed nodded. "Right." He opened the car door and stepped into the cold night, closed it softly, then looked to Patrick, who was grinning. *Damn fool.* On the other hand, the wolf appeared far more alert and ready than Reed felt. "Go."

Together they charged across the street, Reed letting his hands turn half to bone as his boots splashed through puddles.

Patrick pulled ahead and leapt at the club's rear door, arm flung back.

He swung with a cry of joy.

Wood splintered with a crack. The entire door crashed into a room cluttered with dormant PA equipment and a small table. Patrick was inside in a flash, growling as he passed through. Reed followed right on the man's heels.

The werewolf was already tossing a thug to the ground, moving on to a second – this man had pulled his gun with a shout. But Patrick was too fast. He knocked the weapon free and caught the fellow by the throat. "Where's Froud?"

The man gasped out the words. "Next room."

"Thanks, mate." Reed bent to scoop up the handgun.

He opened the door to find Froud in a dim office, half-risen from a ledger at his desk.

His eyes widened when he saw Reed and he hit the floor, cringing beneath the table. Reed leapt closer, gun raised – but the man wasn't going for a weapon, he was breathing hard. "I'm asking this once, Mr Froud," Reed said as he frowned down. "How do I find your hired killer?"

Froud gaped, mouth like a fish. "But I already gave you the number."

"I'll need more."

"That's the way we've always done business, please, I swear." He cringed back further. "I just can't have you do it to me again."

Reed glared at the man. *Exactly what I was afraid of.*

"Reed, I think you should come in here," Patrick said, his voice unworried.

Reed held out a hand, keeping the bone visible as he did. "Give me your phone."

Froud fumbled the mobile free and handed it over, eyes wide.

"Stay under your desk."

A trembling nod.

Reed returned to the next room, where the first thug had found his feet, hands raised where he'd pressed his back against the wall, a broken print of Cold Chisel beside him. The thug was the same guy who'd attacked Reed at the golf course.

"I can help you," he said quietly, glancing at Reed's hands with a shudder. "But I'll want something in return."

"How?" Reed said. He glanced at Patrick, who'd already lowered the hopefully only-unconscious second thug.

"I know how to find the guy you want but I can't tell you unless you help," he said, keeping his voice low. "I just need you to make it look like I died here, okay? Then I'll take you to Robert."

"Robert?"

He nodded. "Name's Dennis and I know Robert because he's my foster brother."

Chapter 13.

Reed blinked. "What?"

The thug's shoulders shook a moment and then he glanced over at the closed door to Froud's office. "Like I said. And that's my terms."

Reed shrugged. "Fine. Got a knife?"

Dennis pulled a blade.

"Let some blood, buddy." Reed lifted the gun, paused to glance at everyone, then fired into the wall.

Dennis cut into his forearm, blood spreading after the point. His expression did not change as he cut himself and he spoke softly. "Whereabouts?"

Reed gestured to the floor and wall near the bullet hole. "Just make it look like you fell against the wall – and quickly."

While Dennis worked, and the man seemed to almost take a painterly approach to the task, Reed flipped through the contacts in Froud's phone, stopping at Alan Dunstall. "Perfect." He took a photo of the contact screen then pulled the battery and sim card from the phone, tossing them behind the piles of cabling and blocky speakers.

Then he wiped the barrel in the blood and fired again, into the blood-stained wall – not much of a forensic counter-measure, but he wasn't going to spend a whole lot of time on it either.

"We about done?" Patrick asked, his eyes still bright.

"I think so." Reed strode to Alan's office and thumped on the door. "Why don't you count to a thousand before you come out, Mr Froud? We'll take care of the body for you."

"Let's escort Dennis to the car then," Reed said to Patrick quietly, who grabbed Dennis by the arm and walked him outside.

They ran through the shadows and leapt into Reed's rental. "Where to then?" he asked as he pulled the car out of the side street, waving at a driver who seemed to be deeply committed to their obscene gesturing.

"Carlton."

"So, Robert's your foster brother?" Reed asked.

Dennis sighed from the backseat. "I suppose you have a joke about how we crooks all know each other?"

"Not really." Even if the word 'crook' sounded a bit like old-school gangster film. *Still, no need to antagonise him.*

"Well, we spent a bit of time in a foster home. Looked out for each other."

Patrick gave a low whistle.

"What's that mean?" Dennis asked.

"Just sounds like you're selling out your brother."

Reed glanced in the mirror. Dennis didn't seem too concerned about the werewolf's observation.

"We're not pals, if that's what you're worried about."

"This feels like quite the change of heart, Dennis," Reed

said before Patrick could continue.

"I suppose it would, yeah."

"You want out – I think that's clear after our little stunt back there. Do you have a plan for after this?"

"You're going to kill Robert, right?"

"If it comes to that," Reed said, even though he didn't truly know.

"Yeah, well, I've been thinking. Ever since you and I... met at the golf course. That... whatever it was, made me take stock a bit." He shrugged. "Might have to run now. New leaf and that is pretty hard for someone like me; no-one wants to hire my sort."

"Maybe that's because–" Patrick began, but Reed cut him off.

Dennis waved a hand. "No, he's right. I didn't start like this – it was gradual, you know? But I was the one that took each step, so that's that."

"What can you tell us about Robert?" Reed said after a moment.

"Not much. I know he's on Cardigan Street in a nice place and that he takes care of the stuff I won't usually touch. Like that girl; she was sweet."

"You met Elise?" Reed asked.

"Just once. She wasn't ready; I think she was more into all that weird shit Dunstall had going on with the bearded guy."

"Treveyos," Reed said.

"Think so."

"That's all you know?"

"Yeah." Dennis leant forward then, pointing as he did. "This is the turn."

The buildings were a mix of new apartments and old

terrace houses, their wrought iron fences dark, matching the mostly bare trees. None had actual front yards and it was an exceedingly regular-looking place; there were even kids chasing a dog around a little park, parents watching from a picnic bench. *The winter coats and steaming breath sort of undercuts the idyllic picture, though.*

"The blue roof," Dennis said.

Reed rode the roundabout then pulled up behind a plumber's van and cut the engine. "And you think he's home?"

Dennis nodded. "He sleeps most of the day and Froud didn't have anything coming up that I'm aware of."

"I assume he works for more than one employer, however," Reed said, still staring at the place. It had a single piece of decoration by the front door, a potted plant of jade in a terracotta pot.

"Right. But now you know where he lives, even if he's not home." The back door clicked open. "Thanks for the lift."

Patrick glanced at Reed, who only shook his head. "Thanks, Dennis," he said. "Keep yourself out of trouble, won't you?"

"I'll do my best," he said with a grunt, then started back down the street, toward a distant pub, it seemed.

"You don't need him anymore?" Patrick asked.

"Probably not," Reed said. "I'm more concerned with what might be inside. I *really* need this guy to have some answers."

"And if not?"

"Then I need to dump him off at a police station."

Patrick made a little sound of disappointment. "Really?"

"Not sure I'm up to murdering anyone today, even a contract killer."

"Then I'll be happy to do it if you change your mind."

"Thanks," Reed said as he exited the car, Patrick joining him. "Let's start with whether he's home." He strode to the rear of the car, opened the boot and pulled out a pair of overalls and a high-vis vest.

"What's our cover then?" Patrick asked as Reed wrestled with the bottoms, kicking his boots through the legs with a grunt.

"Concerns with a gas leak."

"Think he'll buy it?"

"Let's find out – whether he does or not, we're going in fast, right?"

Patrick grinned again. "Right."

"Patrick, you might be having too much fun."

"Come on, don't spoil it for me."

Chapter 14.

Robert the hit-man had a nondescript wooden front door and a tidy step. Reed rapped on the wood and waited.

No answer.

Patrick shrugged his shoulders, as if getting ready to strike.

Reed knocked again, harder. Anger was already building. This was the bastard who'd killed Elise and the prick wasn't even home?

And still nothing from within the terrace house. Maybe Robert was sleeping, maybe he was out – either way, the ruse would only work if the guy actually came to the door.

"Sir, this is important," Reed shouted as he knocked again. "You may have to evacuate."

"Fuck off!" came a reply.

Patrick snickered.

Reed knocked again, harder still. "This is serious. We're from the gas company, sir."

Footsteps thundered up a passage but the door didn't open. "I said, 'fuck off', got it, dipshit?"

Reed glanced over his shoulder – no-one was walking

the street and the family in the park didn't seem to be paying attention. He stepped aside and nodded to Patrick.

Almost bouncing upon his toes, Patrick skipped back, then charged.

The door burst inward, soaring from its hinges.

Hard wood slammed into a figure within a dim hall. The man shouted in shock and pain, but Patrick was upon him instantly, hauling the man up by the neck of his shirt and shoving him into the nearest room.

Reed dashed after.

The first room was a small lounge. It contained a couch that faced a dark TV in shelving, though rows and rows of books lined the rest of the room. Robert was a balding man who seemed in good shape, his dark brows set in a deep frown as he struggled against Patrick's grip, who'd switched to a headlock upon the couch.

Reed stood over the two. "Froud paid you to kill Elise Roberts, a teenage runaway, on behalf of Dunstall."

"Get fucked, pig," Robert said with a snarl.

Reed chuckled. "I'm not a cop, as you'll soon see." He looked to Patrick. "Can you break his collarbone from that position?"

"Hmmm." Patrick clucked his tongue. "I'll give it a shot."

"Please do."

He flexed and a crunch followed.

Robert screamed.

"I think we've got time for a few more bones if you need to think," Reed said.

Robert only glared up at him, breathing heavily – as best he could.

"I'll take your silence as confirmation that you're the

correct Robert, at least," Reed said. He glanced to Patrick. "Put him to sleep if he refuses again."

"For how long?"

"Long enough to search the place while he naps."

"Not, you know... for longer?"

Reed knelt down before the snarling Robert. "We'll see." He opened himself to the Fringe and let his face become skull-like, the Reaper side of him coming to the fore.

The assassin flinched, eyes widening to almost perfect circles.

But Reed paused at an odd scent, one that seemed to have forced its way into the room.

Like smouldering sand.

He spun out of his crouch but the room was empty... yet the smell, how was it familiar?

Gods, it's like home, back when Mum and Dad disappeared!

"What's wrong?" Patrick asked.

"Something's here," Reed replied, taking a step toward the hall.

The sizzle of burning sand flared behind him. Reed whirled as a figure rose from behind the couch. A spindly thing, it was somehow colourless, yet the faceless lump of a head bore a radiant crown – like Helios of Greece but they were not rays so much as flesh with blackened tips...

Reed flinched back, and though it did not touch him, the *feel* of it crossed the room.

As though worms filled his mouth and more, like something papery and cold brushing up against any part of exposed skin.

Patrick had shrunk back too, still holding the now frozen hit-man.

"What are you?" Reed demanded.

The thing turned its eyeless face his way, limbs flicking up to hover over Patrick and Robert. *I believe these will be useful.*

Sharp fingers snapped and the couch lay empty.

Reed took another step back.

The thing still regarded him, unmoving, featureless. *All work and no fun, yes?*

And then it was gone, taking with it the smell of searing sand and the sensation of being caressed by sickly, chill paper.

"Hey!"

Reed wheeled on the empty room, then leapt to the couch but all was 'normal' once more. He exhaled. *What the fuck was that thing?*

It had to be the same as whatever took his parents... didn't it?

Why had it come?

And the quip about all work and no play – had the thing that stole Feronia's hand been behind the disappearance of his parents? How was that even possible?

But it was gone now.

And it took Patrick and Robert, but why? Would *their* knuckle bones soon appear? "Shit." *I'm out of my depth here.* He raised his voice. "Max? Lina?"

No answer.

"Valen, I need to speak to you." Now he shouted. "Even Potter will do!"

Lina appeared on the couch, legs and arms crossed, with a small frown. "Reed, what's happening?"

"Can you sense it?"

She stood. "What?"

"*Something* was here. It took two people. I think it was the same thing that took my parents."

"Really?" She sniffed at the air. "I mean, maybe a trace of something... it's not..."

The faint sound of bells echoed, and then Valen, Potter and Max appeared – each of their faces wearing an expression of concern. "Describe this thing, Reed," Potter said, scythe in hand.

"Thin and featureless. It had a radiant crown but the prongs were like blackened flesh." He shook his head. "When it spoke there was no voice, in the human sense. It brought the smell of burning sand or maybe ancient dust. Like with my parents."

Potter's stern eyes looked around at those gathered. "Anyone?"

"Nothing I know of, brother," Valen said.

"I will ask Mother," he said. "The rest of you, ask around – quickly."

Then he was gone.

Valen smiled, almost sadly, and then he too disappeared.

Max sighed. "I don't like the sound of this, Cousin. It's not good if Potter isn't aware of it."

"No."

He clasped his hands behind his back. "I'll check on Pluto and see if he knows anything."

"Right."

And then only Lina remained. She was pacing the room now. "I know what Potter said but I think I'll stay with you a little longer."

"Won't that anger Aunty?" Reed asked, though Lina's presence was welcome indeed.

"Doubtless, but what doesn't? I don't know if she has ever laughed."

"And what about the doll?"

She waved a hand. "I've left it sleeping – they moved you to solitary, five days."

He blinked. What sort of trouble would that bring later? "What did I do?"

"Oh, you know just a bit of refusal to comply with a request. The guard was just in a bad mood, to be honest. But let me think a minute, Reed."

"What do you have in mind?"

"I don't know. I should be able to sense that thing – we all should, yet there's only truly faint traces... It's as though they're hidden, woven into things that are natural." She sighed. "Was there anything else?"

All work and no fun, yes?

"A quote but..." he trailed off. Did that mean Emma was in danger? He crossed the room and gripped Lina's shoulders. "Can you check on Emma for me?"

"Minerva's girl?"

"At the library, yes."

"I can, but –"

"That thing might have gone after her for some reason, maybe the Book of Hours, I don't know but she translated the message it left behind. She could be in danger."

"All right."

"And be careful," he added, but she'd disappeared before he'd finished speaking.

Despite the fear-fuelled adrenaline that now ran through him, he could hardly reach Emma as quickly as Lina – better that he let *her* check, and while he waited, try to find some damn evidence related to Elise's case.

Reed looked back at the couch once more... nothing.

Back in the hall, he could see right into the street, courtesy of the still-shattered door. *Pick up the pace, who knows if any neighbours heard Robert scream.* At the end of the hall lay a neat kitchen, coffee waiting by a silver kettle. Beyond, laundry. Far more spartan. Back in the hall he found a study beside the bedroom, silent laptop waiting on a desk. A three-drawer filing cabinet blocked part of a window and Reed gave it a kick as he pulled on black gloves.

Locked.

He rifled through a few drawers but aside from stationary and take-away menus, there was no key. *It'd be easier to take the computer and go digging around there.*

Providing he could crack the password.

"Reed?"

Lina from the other room.

He lifted the laptop and held it behind his back. "In here."

"Emma's fine. I thought I'd locked on to your exact location, you know..." she trailed off when she appeared at the doorway. "Ah."

"The laptop?" he asked.

She shrugged. "Sometimes electronics interfere a little."

"I'm hoping you don't fry the thing, you know."

"Less likely while it's turned off, though I suppose Mother would have ruined it by now."

"So was Emma well?"

Lina nodded with a small smile. "She was. No visitors. But she wants to see you, actually."

"All right, I'll go over–"

"For dinner, Reed. She's going to be at your place at seven."

"Oh."

Lina winked. "Like a date."

He hesitated; it was too much to process in the moment. He still half-expected the thing to return. "You think so?"

"Call it a dead girl's intuition."

"Then I'll go and get started on this laptop," he said. A kind of muted excitement had begun to return from somewhere, very faint for now. "What will you do?"

"Sniff around here a little longer. Maybe I'll find a trail."

He hesitated. "Is that safe?"

"I think whatever it was is long gone," Lina said. "I know what to watch for, now that I've sensed it."

"But still..."

"Listen to your elders, Reed," she said then, her voice hardening, and he caught a glimpse of the ancient being beneath the somewhat pixie-like facade, something she rarely shared. "It will not surprise me."

Chapter 15.

In the warmth of his lounge, Reed snapped the lid of the stolen laptop closed with a huff. Still no luck. *And now you're running out of time for dinner.* He had to make sure he tidied up before Emma arrived.

He started by collecting music magazines and empty cups, and then paused. He shook his head.

If you don't really believe Lina, why clean up?

But he still arranged a few things, since it was a welcome distraction from the simmering anger that had not fully faded – he'd lost a good lead in Robert. And Patrick had to be saved too.

Somehow.

In the kitchen, Reed opened the window to try and deal with some of the stuffiness. He was shivering by the time he'd started cooking; browning meat and adding sauce, then stirring in some salt, pepper and Worcestershire sauce. Nice to actually focus on a meal, to spend time on something so *normal*, considering the last few weeks.

And it feels good to do it for someone else too.

Not that he'd been feeling lonely precisely... but then, having his cousins drop in at various times, often unannounced, was hardly a healthy social life, either. Nor was it conducive to any sort of romantic relationship with a normal person.

The sauce splattered and he eased the heat and stirred again.

Still time to let it settle before she arrived, thankfully.

When there was a knock on the door sometime later, the pasta was nearly ready. He hurried to open the door.

Emma smiled as she entered, handing him a coat. "Whatever you're cooking smells great," she said. She wore jeans and a red sweater, the combination simple and eye-catching.

At least, it certainly works for me.

"Thanks," he said. "Take a seat while I dish up if you like."

Emma did so, leaning back a little. "I was surprised that you sent Lina to check up on me."

He shrugged as he strained the pasta. "That thing was nothing to take lightly – it snatched up my suspect and a werewolf like it was picking up a couple of ornaments."

"Well, I am not defenceless, myself."

He suppressed a sigh as he ladled meat onto the pasta. *Things were suddenly going poorly.* "Is that a not-so-subtle way of telling me that I'm interfering?"

"Maybe."

He placed the plates down, noting with a small smile that Emma had swapped the order of fork and knife where they'd been arranged on the table. "Okay. What about the message or the book, has anything changed?"

"That's why I wanted to see you tonight. A new phrase

appeared and I think it's somehow worse."

"Wonderful."

"I've translated it as something like the Chinese proverb: 'a frog in a well cannot conceive of the ocean', but the way the words appeared... I don't know, it seemed smug. Almost a threat, even."

Reed lowered his fork. "That's not good."

"Yes. Especially since we are no doubt the frogs."

He sighed. "Well, thanks. Even if it is bad news, it's good to slowly form a picture of what we're up against. Did you tell Minerva?"

"Yes. She's spread it around."

"Good, that saves me a job, at least."

They continued the meal but by the end, Emma had stood to take her dishes to the sink with a troubled expression. He joined her. "Let me, you're the guest after all."

"Very kind," she said, moving aside to lean against the sink with a smile. But it did not last. "You haven't actually told me about the thing itself."

"Think you'd maybe recognise it?" The imagined scent of hot sand returned.

"It'd help if I can, right?"

He nodded. "It wasn't fully visible somehow... I mean, I could see it, and it was gangly but not that solid, I guess. It didn't have a face, more of a lump. The colour of its skin didn't seem to be anything. It's hard to describe, but the thing was still very present in the room." He paused. "More than that, I remember the radiant crown."

"A radiant crown?"

"Yeah. Made out of flesh. And the tips were black, as

though it had been burnt. It made me think of a Helios but I doubt this is anything from the Greek Pantheon."

Emma's frown had deepened. "Nor I. Anything else?"

"Like with my parents, I could smell what seemed to be burning sand."

"Oh."

"But no runes appeared. Instead, I felt like worms and paper were sliding across my skin."

She straightened. "Worms?"

"The more I think about it the more disgusting it seems. Why?"

"Something about that *is* familiar." She skipped toward the door, grabbing her coat as she did. "I think I need to do some research, Reed. Next time it's my turn to cook, okay?"

"Sounds good," he said, and she was already at the door, waving almost before he'd finished his words.

He blinked. *That was fast.*

And then he chuckled, despite the lingering worry. Emma had not changed; she still leapt, almost literally, into her research.

He finished cleaning up before flicking the television on and opening up Robert's laptop once more, though he quickly closed it again. There was no point really, not after his rudimentary attempts to break in had been rebuffed several times. Better to use a professional. *And I know exactly who to ask too.*

A roar from the TV-crowd caused him to glance up; someone was winning a tennis match, the late night game beaming in all the way from Wimbledon. Reed set the laptop on the coffee table then leant back in the armchair...

... and woke to a knocking upon his door.

He struggled upright, blinking. *What time was it?*

The TV had slid into infomercials now, one of them bubbled away about forty-seven ways to use a torch. The knock came again as he pushed himself from the chair, approaching softly. Had Emma forgotten something?

"Unlikely."

After all, it was pretty late.

And the trouble with assumptions holds true with late night visitors just as much as it does during cases.

He had an almost paranoid range of wards up – both on the building and around apartment itself, but those weren't aimed at humans.

At the door he paused, holding the handle but pressing himself up against the wall instead. "Calling a little late, aren't we?"

"Reed?" The voice wavered, sounding close to tears.

A woman... but not Emma. And not a familiar voice at all. He frowned as he pulled the door open.

The dark-haired woman wore a heavy trench coat of black and mascara had run from reddened eyes.

"Lily?"

She swallowed as she nodded. A sports bag rested at her feet. "I couldn't find you... I couldn't remember properly."

"Shit, come inside, please," he said, closing the door after her. "Sit in the kitchen; I'll make you a drink."

Lily did so, shoulders trembling as she fought back tears.

He set the kettle to boiling, then hesitated. Lily *looked* like she was 30-odd but in some ways she wasn't so old. "Do you even like coffee?"

"Not really."

He found some juice in the fridge but didn't stop the kettle, since he definitely needed something to make him a little sharper.

"What happened?" he asked gently as he handed the glass over and sat.

She took a long drink then met his eyes, her gaze despondent... haunted even. "I don't know. It doesn't make sense."

"What doesn't?"

"I tried to visit them. But I couldn't make myself knock on the door."

"Your family?"

"Yeah."

"At least you know they're well," he said.

She nodded. "I saw them though... they're suddenly a lot older, Reed."

He placed a hand over hers. "One day, I could visit with you, if you like?"

Lily hung her head. "I don't know. I'm... it's weird. I'm me but this isn't my body. And I feel like shit because I ran away from her family; they don't even know. They call me Jane. Sometimes I don't even turn around at first and then I see the hurt on their faces..."

Reed tensed at a wave of guilt, his stomach twisting. Hard. "But you came here?"

She looked up, eyes still swollen from tears. "No-one else would understand."

He squeezed her hand now. "You can visit me any time. Talk to me any time, Lily."

"Thanks," she said, almost a whisper. "I don't want to hurt them, you know? They're such nice people and they were so happy to see Jane but I can't act like their daughter... so I thought maybe it was best if I left. I don't want to trash their memories. Do you think they'd be happy if I ran away? They'd know I was alive, at least. Not stuck in that hospital."

He hesitated. What answer could he possibly give?

"Come on, tell me what you think." She straightened. "My idea makes sense, doesn't it?"

"Well, it's sort of logical..."

"But?"

"I think you know what I'm going to say."

Her shoulders slumped. "I guess so."

"If you do go back, why don't you tell them that you can't remember much and that it's hard. Let them know you need a bit of space. If you can say it calmly, they'll probably understand. Maybe hug them too. I know if I had a daughter and I thought I'd lost her, I'd appreciate it even if she seemed confused."

Lily smiled and pushed dark hair from her face. "You're not too bad at this, Reed."

"Ah, thanks."

"Seriously." She took another drink, then glanced back at the couch. "So, ah... is it all right if I stay here tonight?"

"It is. Why don't you take the bathroom and I'll sort out the sofa bed."

"Okay." She took her bag and strode down the hall, wiping at her cheeks.

Reed turned to the sofa bed with a slight frown – and not simply because the thing was predictably temperamental, but because of a sudden urge to double check the wards he'd put in place, to make sure the door was truly locked.

Everything was different for tonight, now that he was responsible for someone else.

Chapter 16.

Reed paced his kitchen, tiles cold beneath his bare feet, note in hand.

Lily had already left, apologising but promising to give her new family more time, which was encouraging at least. Following her might have been an option but in the end, he couldn't justify it, surely? Maybe she wanted to face the difficult adjustment herself now that she'd had some time… but he could check on her tomorrow or later in the day.

And if she asks again – I'll help.

Instead, he had to rescue Patrick and Robert. *One because I'm responsible for getting him into the mess.* And the other because he was the best damn witness still alive. "Hopefully."

The laptop could be dropped off at Caitlyn's shop but while she got to work, the underground beckoned. And this time, he couldn't risk getting anyone else tangled up in the trouble. Not even Max or Lina – not that Aunty would agree even if he requested they help. No, he had to protect them too.

Who knew what the thing could do?

Reed strode to his bedroom, pulled open the cupboard and drew free the chest with the bone form of the Coda, and then the one behind it, where he pulled out a black tunic with the Roman Numerals for 'thirteen' emblazoned across the chest in silver.

Would it make much difference? Hard to know; it was only really good against a few subsets of demons but unlike his last trip involving the Fringe, this time it seemed like old customs and ancient rituals couldn't hurt. Especially since, this time, he probably wouldn't be given a mark from Mors...

"Or would I?"

Reed slipped the tunic into a backpack then headed for the bathroom where he filled the sink. Then, he ducked back to the bedside table and found a ten-cent piece, which he flipped into the water. "With this token I call upon Mors," he said. "Let her hear my mortal voice, a whisper across water."

Lights flickered and her skeletal but somehow indistinct visage appeared within the mirror, hollow sockets conveying... irritation?

"What is amiss now, Reed?"

"Everything," he replied with a frown. "I'm heading underground to follow up on a clue related to whatever stole Feronia's hand and I might need to enter the Fringe."

"And you wish for a Mark."

"Yes."

A dusty sigh. "Very well." Bones reached through the glass to sketch the black noose before him. It blazed then faded, and then she seemed to narrow her eyes. "Is that all?"

"Not really, no. Do you know what I might be facing

down there? Has Minerva or Lina described the thing I saw?"

"Yes. It is... not precise."

"Meaning?"

"Meaning that we do not understand what it is yet. Perhaps your investigation will uncover more useful information."

"At what cost?"

"That we do not know, as yet. But I believe you are able to handle this, Reed. Adieu."

Her image flickered away and the lights returned to a steady glow.

"Shouldn't that have been 'arrivederci', Aunty?"

Reed shook his head. Had her compliment actually been sincere?

Of course, there'd been no emotion in the words – there never was – but on one hand she didn't seem concerned that he might not survive bringing any possible new information to light, on the other hand... maybe she truly *did* think he could handle himself.

Flattery and manipulation?

Or her best effort at encouragement?

Impossible to tell. And the fact that there was another 'half-skull' out there lingered in his mind too; it added to her refusal to let Max and Lina become too involved and reinforced the idea that he was, if not disposable precisely, it was at least possible to replace him.

But that was truly a problem for another day.

He ran a bath and filled the warm water with amber oil, dipped himself in and dried off before dressing and retrieving his Mexican Glass Butterfly Ring. Sonorus was coming along, but there was one more shop he'd visit – and hurrying wasn't such a bad idea either.

Next on his list was Robert's laptop. That was heading to Caitlyn's repair shop.

By the time he'd reached his car he was breathing a little hard.

Excitement or fear?

Bloody hell, it better not be both.

The road was not too busy and he reached *Motherboard Electronics* soon enough, taking the laptop through the rows of accessories to the counter, where a young lad wearing a purple polo, with his name 'Steve' upon it, accepted the computer. "Another one for Caitlyn?" the man asked. "She's not in but I'll make sure she gets it this afternoon, if you like?"

"Yep. Thanks. It's not urgent but it is sensitive," he said, offering the usual warning. No good if Caitlyn or her staff were dragged into something, though she knew her business more than well enough.

"Right. I'll get her to call you, Mr Lavender."

"Thanks." Reed headed back to his rental and then started on a somewhat more tedious trip across the city, this time to the eastern suburbs, toward Glen Waverley where Zhou Jun's Antiques was tucked away above a childcare centre.

Upon first meeting Jun, Reed had asked about the centre, about the danger. The man had only shrugged and replied, "My customers know exactly what will come of them should they interfere."

And he hadn't explained, but that lack of explanation was intimidating enough on its own.

More, considering the things the man had found over

the years, Reed had soon come to agree that crossing Jun was certainly a mistake.

When Reed arrived, Jun was adding salt to a row of dishes of rice and chicken lain out upon a kitchen table. *Cooking for the staff again, no doubt.* The smell was enough to make his mouth water – he'd skipped breakfast and lunch.

"Come in, Reed." The man looked up from his work with a smile. "I haven't seen you in a little while. Planning something stupid?"

"Probably."

He finished up and gave a shout toward the other rooms, then waved Reed toward a second door – this one leading to a narrow corridor and at the end, a workshop of benches littered with tools and boxes, lamps beaming overhead. The walls were covered in hanging tools or posters of gourmet meals from all over the world.

"I've been holding on to something for months now," Jun said as he rummaged around beneath one of the chipped workbenches. He lifted a steel chest up and set it down with a thump. "Take a look."

Reed opened the lid and pulled forth something wrapped in black velvet. It seemed to grow heavier as he unwrapped... a short sword, specifically, a Gladius. The edges were undulled, the knobbed hilt dark and clean. The grip bore grooves for fingers, smooth as he lifted it. The blade bore no ornamentation; it simply was.

If it was a replica, it seemed very fine indeed.

Yet if it was an authentic antique, then it was a miraculous triumph of steel over decay.

"This feels... special," he said.

"It is. It was uncovered in the Sahara, years ago now. Since then, it's been moving between dealers. When I got my hands on it I set it aside for you."

"Wow." Reed examined the blade again. Not a single notch or mark. And the weight of it, while light overall, was heavier than natural. Why? There was more; that unclear sense that it was special somehow. Without his gun, and with perhaps no need for one, having a blade might not hurt at all – since when it came to surprises underground, there was at least a chance it would be useful in both the regular world and perhaps the Fringe. "What do you know about it?"

"Not that much. The history of ownership doesn't offer much info but I can say no-one seemed to keep it longer than a year." He scratched at his head. "Last guy didn't know why. I've been trying to find out more but if you take the sword I can hand that task over to you."

"Hmmm."

"Want to barter?"

"Well, I did come hoping to find a weapon of some sort."

"Perfect."

"This set you back, didn't it?"

Jun nodded. "And since I know you're not rolling in cash, what do you think about a favour?"

"I owe a lot of those, right now," Reed said, apprehension building.

"I'm not surprised to hear that," he replied with a grin. "But what I've got in mind is a big one."

Reed put the blade back in the chest, where a scabbard waited. Convenient. "Hit me with it, Jun. You know I'll do my best."

"I do, but this one isn't for me precisely. It's for a friend,

Eddie – he wants to speak to a loved one."

"Ah." Reed didn't sigh – what Jun asked was against the rules, rules Reed himself had recently broken and landed himself in hot water by doing so. "I can pass a message on, no problem."

"I appreciate that, and I know you've done something similar before on my behalf but this time I think we need an actual conversation. Can you make that happen?"

"I can." *Somehow.*

"Good, thank you."

"Your friend isn't in any hurry, I hope?"

"No. I just thought I'd be able to help, since I know you."

Reed nodded. "Let me deal with a little problem first, though it might take a while."

Chapter 17.

Once more, Reed found himself squeezing between walls in the dim underground, slipping in and out of the Fringe, light from his torch revealing more chipped stone but most importantly, a blackened, faintly pulsating trail of slime.

The slime trail led him deeper along the wide tunnels to more walls; some of which his quarry had tunnelled through the stone and earth, while with others it seemed to have passed beyond, like the spirit worm.

This is the right trail. It had to be, for there was nothing else like it beneath Robert the hit-man's home and no other creature he knew of left a snail-like trail of dark, faintly hissing goo.

And it was no spirit-worm either; something he knew each time he opened himself up to the Fringe. It was clear what the creature had done. Dozens of grey 'rips' in the underground suggested the thing was passing through the Fringe without much control.

He followed it still.

In the Fringe, each step within the grey, ash-choked ruin

of stone walls offered the usual oppressive heat, but no hints of the usual denizens. Not unheard of at all... but then, if something so powerful had come, had it scared off the regular inhabitants of the Fringe?

A sound echoed from the passage ahead and he slowed.

What was it? A faint, brass-like glow joining the indistinct sound. He checked on Sonorous and then the Gladius where it hung over his tunic – hard not to feel a little like an actor in a sword and sandal epic or a fantasy film.

The real question is, will any of it be enough for what's ahead?

Whatever the sound was – it seemed like earth and stone trickling down now – he could not back away. Whether it was something unknown, like whatever had chased Devin, or more like the sand-fiend with its Radiant Crown of blackened flesh, someone had to deal with it and then, someone had to save Patrick and Robert.

"Which means me."

Yet Reed could not take the next step.

Just how serious is this?

He ground his teeth and smacked a fist against his thigh. "Come on, you owe Elise too."

His foot finally moved and he strode forward now, one hand on the hilt of his blade and the other gripping the torch, perhaps a little too hard. A sick feeling grew in his stomach as he approached the glow.

The light revealed a large cavern, its walls slick with dark slime.

And in its centre waited a tall creature, its body wide as an elephant, its arms outstretched.

The thing was a shadowy shape but glints of more human-toned flesh appeared beneath the dark skin, like thin tears where its long arms reached up and up to the stony ceiling – a spindly thing that gave off an ugly sensation, like squirming worms filling his mouth or paper hands caressing skin.

Reed gagged.

But the sound did not disturb his target at all; the foul being simply worked on, digging up toward the surface if the trail of falling earth was any indicator. Somehow, by accident or choice, it had missed the occasional pipe or electrical trench... so as not to draw attention to itself? Reed squinted but the head remained concealed by raised arms.

Something else caught his eye – flecks of grey also filled the cavern. Yet all around the open area stood bulging distortions in the very stone and earth.

As if other things were trying to push through.

Fringe-dwellers?

It was *extremely* rare for even a single creature from beyond to try passing through without taking advantage of a poorly constructed summoning circle or similar, and now multiple things were trying to simply push through all at once in the one place?

Reed tore Sonorous free and leapt into the cavern, where he snapped his wrist.

A clear note rang out.

Shapes flinched back as if from a gunshot and the cavern walls grew smooth, natural once more. A few creatures, probably White Hunters, remained behind, straining against the unseen barrier, but he rang the bell once more and each one receded.

So too, the tall thing twitched violently.

Reed rang Sonorous again and now the creature flinched, limbs shivering down to reveal a lumpy face with a now familiar Radiant Crown of black.

"Shit."

Reed gave ground but the creature charged, limbs aflutter, like disgusting liquid flesh. Its voice rang in his mind, instantly forgettable in both tone and tenor.

Another interruption.

The thing leant in close and the scent of burning sand seared Reed's nose and throat.

He dropped his torch and tore the Gladius free, slashing as he did. The blade cut into one of the creature's limbs – a shallow wound only, and black bile sprayed forth, splashing over him. Reed gave a shout as the bile burned his skin, and shielded himself with an arm, stumbling to smack into the wall.

But he could not move now, his limbs were stiffening.

It was already looming over him once more, dripping its slimy blood.

Light flashed.

The thing reared back, arms flailing – it should have been vaguely amusing, but it wasn't; the whole scene remained disturbing, as the empty face revealed no expression, the whole lump making not a single sound.

Reed blinked.

Max and Lina stood before him, both blazing with a silvery light. "Back!" Max shouted.

The light unfroze Reed's limbs and he straightened.

Yet the mute face drew near once more, the body still not moving, and opened its mouth. Another stream of inky bile burst forth to splash across Max and Lina. Their light dimmed and before Reed could even duck away – both were frozen as stone statues.

"No!"

They'd protected him.

Still the creature did not recede. He tensed, but rang the Sonorous once more and the note echoed around the cavern, causing the horror to shiver. It weaved in the air a moment and then began to shudder harder, the head and arms... deflating, as it shrunk down swiftly to a pile of slush.

The feeling of worms disappeared, so too the brass-glow and the scent of sand.

Had just one more note been enough, after the light?

And is it truly gone?

He did not sense it near – but nor did he put the Sonorous away.

Reed dashed around to face Max and Lina but they had not changed. The bell had not sent them away; they were two perfect statues. He reached out to place a hand on Max's shoulder, glancing to Lina's fierce expression. *They broke Aunty's rules and saved me themselves.*

Yet how could be possibly return the favour?

He raised his voice. "Aunty!"

Water or a coin was always a better way to reach her quickly, but he needed help either way, if it wasn't already coming.

There was no answer.

And yet, he had not been wrong either, since a voice soon hailed him from the opening to the cavern.

"We'll take them for you, Half-Skull."

A line of Pluto's grubs were filing in, like sturdy little

soldiers in the darkness, which for anyone else would have rendered the grubs invisible.

"Aunt Mors sent you?"

The speaker seemed to be Rhubarb. "She asked the master, yes."

Reed exhaled, a little tension dissolving. "Thank you all," he said as they surged forward to surround and then lift the stone versions of his cousins.

Chapter 18.

Reed paced a concrete strip before a statue of this or that historical figure, the chill afternoon air doing nothing to lift the mood of the city gardens. Not too far over Valen's shoulder waited glimpses of the state gallery and its silent water features, but Reed found himself glancing around not for landmarks but for any sign of the *thing* that had frozen Max and Lina.

"It has to be an actual god," he said. "Like... like a Radiant King."

"Reed, slow down," Valen replied, voice gentle. He sat upon a nearby park bench, legs crossed, his immaculate blonde hair undisturbed by the breeze.

Reed continued to pace, slightly slower now. "We have to do something."

"Mother is already sending someone to help."

"She can't fix this herself?"

Valen sighed. "I wish it were so –, but whatever that thing was down there, God or Subordinate, its work is troubling."

"Then who's going to help us?"

"Well, I've been told that someone is coming to help you."

Reed stopped. "Aunty is blaming me? I went alone, you know that –"

Valen lifted a hand. "I do. And I don't believe she is assigning any blame. But the person who can help us asked for you specifically."

"Me?"

"Yes. He'll be here soon; I think he believes you can first assist him with something."

"So I'm further into debt then?" he snapped.

"It's for Max and Lina, Reed."

"Sorry," Reed said, raising both hands. "I know. I just can't do everything at once. And some of it, maybe not at all."

"Let's see what Dionysus has to say."

"What?"

"Yes, I sense him approaching – that's who it is, apparently."

"Not Bacchus?"

Valen shrugged once more. "Sometimes, you know I can hardly tell the difference between them myself."

A tall, *classically* handsome man popped into existence on the seat beside Valen. He sat in white robes and sandals, wreath upon his brow – yet a bright pink scarf tied around his neck marred the mythological image. His curls reached his shoulders and his smile was a beaming beacon, almost painfully so. It wasn't just the power of his beauty but a force that exuded from him. Similar but different to Aunty; Dionysus wasn't short-circuiting things but instead the air seemed a little brighter and warmer, the problems he faced a little smaller.

"Valen, you're looking wonderful, my boy."

Valen inclined his head. "Kind of you to say so, Lord Dionysus."

The God winked then hopped up to extend a hand toward Reed. "Join me for a meal, Mr Lavender. I have a proposition for you."

"Ah..."

Dionysus was suddenly directly before him, warm hand gripping his own – and then Reed found himself seated across from the God somewhere else, white tablecloth bearing two glasses of sparkling white wine. The room was a circle of windows, a vast blue ocean beyond, the warm sun pouring through a glittering skylight above.

The God waved a hand in the air and a young woman with dark hair and a neck-to-toe robe of green appeared, twin plates of brightly coloured but oddly-shaped fruit in hand. She set the food down with a smile and then disappeared.

"Please, eat," the god said, his voice like a choir somehow, the warmth that exuded from the man intensifying. "We can talk once you are comforted."

Reed opened his mouth to offer a polite refusal, but he could not speak, and the emptiness in his stomach pushed its way to the forefront, swift and sharp. When *had* he last eaten? The meal was light yet filling, each flavour familiar as it was new and surprising, and it did not take long to finish.

When he looked up, Dionysus had finished his own plate and held his wine glass. "You are no doubt most curious about what I can offer."

"I am, My Lord."

The god waved a hand, as if to dismiss the honorific. "Have you heard of the Lycurgus Cup?"

"I think so. It's an artefact, the cage cup with the colour-changing glass?"

"Precisely. Forged in the fourth century. The glass is green when light strikes from the front and red from the rear. A true work of art indeed, a fitting tribute to my Ambrosia. It currently resides within the British Museum but I would have no objection to ducking over to borrow it."

Reed skipped over the comment about 'ducking over' and asked, "And you think it can restore Max and Lina?"

"I believe it worth an attempt – if it is filled with the right water, I think it will free your cousins."

"I would appreciate that, truly. I feel responsible for what happened."

The god spread his hands. "No-one believes that you are to blame. Even old Jupiter was impressed that you survived. For you see, that thing – the Radiant King as I believe you have already dubbed it – has stolen Feronia's hand and it is no minor demon. Still, we cannot fathom it but what seems clear is that it moves slowly, and from that fact springs our hope."

Reed frowned. "But, surely I'm not the only one standing against it?"

"No, we are still at work here. But so long as this Radiant King continues to act in the mortal plane then mortals will have to respond – you are not alone there, either, of course."

"Are you sending someone to help me?"

"Perhaps, but firstly I think we will restore your cousins." He paused to place his glass upon the tablecloth. "However,

I do require something in return."

"Something I can deliver?"

He leant closer with a nod, and his expression changed from welcoming to one of sternness. "Indeed. You must not arrange for Livius to be revived, as you have previously promised Sol Invictus."

"I..." Reed met the God's amber eyes – a difficult task. "That is your price?"

"Yes."

"It puts me in a difficult position."

"Yes."

Reed shook his head after a moment. "Of course, I have no choice – I am dragged yet deeper into your struggles."

"But you save your cousins, and in doing so, please both your Aunt and me, do you not?"

"And Sol Invictus?"

"I am sure Jupiter will intervene should you succeed in dealing with Feronia's lost hand." He shrugged. "Or perhaps your Aunt will vouch for you."

Reed wasn't so sure at all, but he could hardly refuse. "What water should I use?"

Dionysus stood. "There is a fountain here that will be suitable. If you wait just a moment, I will have the Lycurgus Cup. Just remember, do not drink from it unless you wish to live for an *unpleasantly* long time, and do not spill it before you reach Maximilian and Lina."

"I understand," Reed said.

"Wonderful," the God replied as he vanished.

Chapter 19.

Reed stood before the window, looking over the ocean as he waited. The surface was impossibly still, a crystalline blue. A few faint tufts of cloud hung across the horizon but no birds were visible, just a beaming sun whose rays were possibly actual lances of gold.

It was unnaturally serene and nothing like it could have existed in the mortal world. In a way, it was as though the god had created an idealised painting – only it was so much more than an image.

"Mr Lavender?"

Reed turned. The woman in green stood nearby, her hair cascading down from the top of her head in curls. She was perhaps even more striking than before, now that the sheer force of Dionysus was absent. Her lipstick matched her dress and the wreath-bracelets she wore.

"Yes?"

"I am Ambrosia," she said with a smile. "I'm sorry to say that there will be a slight delay, I hope you understand."

"Ah, of course," he said, after a moment's hesitation.

Time insofar as gods were concerned remained quite nebulous, but it likely meant that the Cup would arrive in *moments* rather than *seconds*. Yet, what remained odd was the deference she offered. "I understand and there's no need to apologise, My Lady. I'm in your master's debt here."

Ambrosia nodded. "Very well. Would you be interested in an observation upon your current troubles?"

"On the Radiant King?"

"Yes. We all discuss it as being old – most suspect that it predates our roles as custodians but that may be misleading."

"How so?"

"Few here care to deeply interrogate the true nature or 'birth' of ourselves. I have come to believe that it may be a comforting construct for us to consider ourselves as being of a certain time, span and role. But I am hardly certain."

"I'm not sure I follow."

"I am suggesting that should you continue on as chief investigator, for lack of a better phrase. Do not assume that the things we tell you are wholly accurate. Or perhaps, it is better to say that not all things translate neatly into human concepts."

He met her gaze. What she said about assumptions certainly made sense but there was something else that caught his attention. "Wait, are the gods thinking of replacing me?"

"I seriously doubt that. You remain useful to them."

"Then, are you hinting that I should... hand off the task to someone else?"

"If the others continue to offer you so little support, then I think you should consider such an option, Reed Lavender." She offered a slight bow, which once again struck Reed as unusual, and then she disappeared.

He wandered back to the table but could not sit.

How unsettling to have his own concerns echoed. *But is she concerned about me while also holding some faith in my abilities... or* warning *me that I'm in over my head?* One prospect was somewhat comforting; though both were troubling in similar ways too. He sighed.

An ornate cup appeared on the tablecloth. Dionysus now sat in the chair opposite. "Here we are. I'll need it back the moment you're done."

Reed lifted the cup. Heavier than he'd expected, it was more like a goblet perhaps, the carving of King Lycurgus being restrained by Ambrosia's vines both clear and detailed, the glass itself green and red when the light changed its colour. "Do I carry the water to Aunt Mors?"

The god shook his head, standing to lead Reed across the room to a fountain that suddenly stood nearby. It was decorated with fauns frolicking amongst grapevines. "No, I believe your cousins are residing in your own home, now." He paused to nod. "Presumably, Mors wants you to speak to them and come up with a way to counter the stone-effect."

"Other than the Cup and your fountain?"

"Yes. But take heart, for I've no doubt such a thing is possible – Minerva is also sending someone to help."

"Glad to hear it," Reed said as he dipped the cage cup within the cool water. In the brief time that the surface engulfed his hand a sense that the water was *alive* washed over him, the sweet coolness clinging. "So do I just–?"

He and Dionysus were already standing in Reed's living room.

Before them, two statues formed perfect images of Max and Lina, their expressions frozen in determination. He turned to Dionysus, who was glancing around the room, taking in a painting of poplars in Florence, a poster of Chris Cornell in his Soundgarden days and beside that, Ronnie James Dio in his signature 'horns up' pose. The god glanced at the old furniture. "Mr Lavender, your dwelling is very modest, is it not?"

"It is," Reed said. "Do you mind if I get started?"

He smiled. "Not at all. Simply pour a few drops upon each of your cousins and they will be restored."

Reed lifted the cup to pour a little water over Max, then Lina, stepping back.

Bright blue and silver spread in wavering lines, like fractures upon the surface of the stone. A sharp cracking followed, and then a shell of stone fell away. It thumped down, quickly joined by other pieces where they all crumbled to dust on his carpet – something to vacuum later.

But more importantly, now Max and Lina stood smiling in full colour.

"Reed!" Lina leapt into his arms as Max slapped him on the back.

"It was thanks to Dionysus, really," he said, disentangling Lina. "And you two saved *me*, remember? That bile would have frozen me too."

Max rubbed at his shoulders. "I wonder if it was slower because you're more human?"

"Possibly."

Max and Lina both thanked the god then, who smiled again. "Of course. Now, I'd better take the cup and be on my way. I hope to see you again, Mr Lavender."

Dionysus reached out for the cup, which Reed offered, then the God blinked out of sight.

Max sighed deeply as he took a seat. "That feels a *lot* better."

"First question has to be exactly what was that thing, right?" Lina asked as she leapt into the other chair.

Reed took the couch with a slow smile. "Right back to it, huh?"

"Well, we never really stopped talking to each other or the others – we were just frozen, is all," he said.

"Really?"

Lina nodded. "It was pretty boring, actually."

"That's just hurtful," Max said with another sigh.

Reed waved his hands. "Hold on. Before you two carry on any more, what did you come up with?"

"That thing down there was like... a limb of whoever is behind it. A little clumsy perhaps, but it's learning and growing in power," Max said.

"We think it hasn't fully formed its true shape, but it sees and acts through the flesh," Lina added. "And I must say; I like your name for it, Reed. The Radiant King. Quite grand but fitting of its menace."

Reed winced at the name. "My pleasure, I suppose. But that all makes sense; otherwise, surely we'd have no chance at stopping it and the Gods would have stepped in themselves."

"Perhaps," Max said.

"Perhaps?"

"Well, I don't know whether I'm right or wrong here – well, whether *Potter* is right or wrong, but he thinks that over the past couple of millennia they're all becoming increasingly... disinterested in the world of humans."

A chill rattled across Reed's bones. *That* was worse than the unfathomable creature itself. "Good to know."

"He could be wrong, Reed," Lina added. "But after being sealed, I think we have to deal with *that* problem before anyone goes down there again."

"Agreed."

"We did figure out one thing at least," Max added. "You know why it was tunnelling up?"

Reed nodded. "I have to assume it's to steal people for whatever purpose it hides from us. That's why I started beneath Phillip's place."

"Right. And maybe while this Radiant King is weak, it simply cannot reach so high in a non-corporal form?" He shrugged, then stretched out, slouching deeper into the armchair. "And there's something else. I think we have a better idea of what's been creating the spirit-worms now – they're appearing where that thing has been."

Reed straightened. "But the worms are a result of human emotion."

"Yes, that's exactly the problem. It only raises more flipping questions, doesn't it?"

"Then... are you saying that the Radiant King... is actually a corrupted human?"

"It could be," Max said. "Certainly it may have once possessed human parts. We simply cannot know yet."

"We spoke to the grubs too," Lina said. "They're going to keep an eye on the site. If another Spirit-worm forms then we know we're on to something."

"It's another clue, at least," Reed said with a nod. "And to be honest, it's not hard to accept the possibility that a human has been used as some sort of surrogate for the true force behind this."

"That's what we need to figure out. Exactly *what* is beyond," Lina said as she rested her chin upon her hand. "What is the Radiant King, truly?"

"So, does this mean Aunty has given you permission to help me properly once more?"

"So long as we come up with a way to counteract being frozen, since Aunty owes Dionysus now, *and* Pluto."

"I know the feeling," Reed said.

Chapter 20.

Reed paced the still-dusty carpet, a glass of milk in hand. It sloshed up the sides, settling whenever he drank or slowed. At one point, he paused to frown down at the small cloud of dust his feet had made. What would milk and spectral dust from a God's bile create together?

Something bad but with calcium, no doubt.

Max and Lina had left to chase down a few theories – which left Emma, who, presumably, had already been sent by Minerva. But she hadn't answered his call and so he waited, unable to calm down as he continued to wonder.

Or maybe worry *is the better word for this.*

He had a long-shot in mind, but it meant using the police... and that wasn't going to be easy. Impossible, more likely. Or at least, impossible until his incarceration was solved.

And perhaps thankfully, Lina revealed that 'he' had been placed in and remained in solitary confinement, while Duong seemed trapped by a combination of red tape and doubt, since he still didn't know who to trust.

At least according to Lina, who had described his state

from her eavesdropping.

Which probably left breaking in to a lab somewhere. There he could test some DNA perhaps, even if that act was the long-shot.

For if one of the grubs could deliver even a hint of useful material, anything that may have scraped off on the cavern's ceiling as the thing tunnelled up, then *maybe* the human surrogate could be identified. That, in turn, might lead to some sort of clue in regard to *how* they were taken and used and finally, by whom.

If the results could be matched to someone already in the system.

And if the results ended up free from whatever taint marred the Radiant King.

He finished the milk. "And assuming whoever the King took had actually been involved in something dark enough that we get another clue."

His phone beeped from the table.

Reed checked the message. Emma was on her way.

This time he only organised drinks while he waited. She arrived with barely a greeting and sat herself once more at the table with him, handing over a large jar of ink, her eyes serious. "Everyone has to keep in mind that this is untested – and more, no-one knows what the Radiant King can do. We're protecting against *one* thing that happened."

Reed nodded as he lifted the ink. "So, you and Minerva approve of the name then?"

"That is what Minerva is calling it, and by 'it' she means the thing *behind* the shell."

"Don't know if I should be proud or not," he said. "So, what do we paint with this?"

"A symbol that I've adapted." She took a pen and a piece of mail – another bill – and sketched on the back of the envelope. It looked vaguely like an Egyptian Ankh but it also bore wings. It bore fewer hard lines too, suggesting movement. "There. For 'Life' but I wanted to get the idea of movement in there, to oppose the idea of being frozen, or trapped stone – hence the wings."

"It's wonderful."

"Thank you," she smiled. "You'll need to use this ink, however. I'm sure your cousins will be able to replicate it themselves, but I think we'll need actual tattoos."

"We?"

Emma nodded, a fierce glint in her eye. "I've been ordered to help. And to be honest, I'm excited. It's been too long since I did something this important."

Reed kept his concern to himself – not that she was incapable, but because it was more of the same old disdain for danger that the gods seemed to have, when it came to mortal lives. "You think we need to get actual tattoos?"

"It'll be a true joining with the body that way. Better for potency, right?"

"True."

"It's also efficient. This ink is special and it's a finite resource, so it doesn't make sense to have to reapply the symbol over and over."

"Good point. What's it made from?"

"Well, it's mostly just regular tattoo ink ingredients, but it also includes a little from Minerva's own ink bottle. I wanted to use her Quill but she thought it might be too dangerous for me. You might have been okay, but she wasn't sure."

"Meaning?"

"It might have slowly transformed us into what was written."

"Oh."

Emma laughed. "Exactly! So, we'll have to come up with a spot for the tattoos *and* find a good artist."

"You going to have to hide yours for work?" Reed asked. While he had no employer to appease, he would probably still keep it from view, generally. Which maybe meant the shoulder or back.

She raised an eyebrow. "How about we figure that out together… in your bedroom?"

Reed blinked.

Emma stood and took his hand, leading him from the kitchen. Reed followed without a word – he was holding his breath like a fool! Not what he'd expected, but already his pulse was skipping more than a few beats.

Emma had already stepped out of her slip-on shoes and know knelt upon his bed. She let his hand go and pulled her shirt over her head, hair falling free. "See any room for some ink?" she asked.

He ran his hands up her sides then parted the hair at the nape of her neck, leaning in to brush his lips across her skin. "Maybe."

Chapter 21.

When he woke to the cold blue of dawn, rain hammering the windows, Emma had already left. But he lay still with a smile, the memory of her skin and hair very clear, like something he could touch if only he cared to really try.

His entire body seemed more alive today – an impressive feat for someone who was at least half dead in some ways. *Maybe you were a little more lonely than you realised.*

Reed rolled onto his side to stretch – and flinched.

Potter stood in his black robe, scythe glinting in the dull light.

"For fuck's sake," Reed snapped. "Can't you ever warn me?"

"I waited until your companion left."

Reed hurled the blankets aside and found his pants, stepping into them but not bothering with a shirt, despite the chill to the air, then strode to the kitchen.

There, he tore a carton of milk from the fridge and poured himself a cup, drinking by the window.

"This is important, Reed."

Potter now stood in the doorway.

"Everything we do is important, right?" Reed replied, shaking his head. "So, what is it, then?"

No answer.

Reed frowned now. Potter appeared to be struggling to speak... his mouth moved and he had begun to blink, hard. He took a faltering step forward.

"Hey, what's wrong?"

The searing scent of sand overwhelmed the kitchen.

Potter's robe burst into shreds. The Reaper split in half as a pale figure grew from the remnants, blackened spikes springing from the lump of a face in the now familiar crown.

Reed leapt back, crashing into the sink. Glass shattered.

The Radiant King opened its mouth and black bile sprayed forth.

Reed raised a hand to shield himself and the bile bounced back, spilling across the floor. The Radiant King thrashed in place, spewing harder, but Reed pushed back. Somehow, he wasn't being encased in stone!

And then it stopped.

The bile was gone, all of it, and the Radiant King too.

Reed lifted his hand, eyes wide, heart still thumping. His palm was a little red, stinging now. "How the hell...?" Could it have been Dionysus' fountain? The water within had clung to his skin.

Somehow, it had been enough today.

But if the stinging after-effect was any indication, he wasn't going to get away with using his hand as a shield next – the tattoo had become suddenly *quite* urgent.

Reed turned back to the doorway, breathing hard. Potter was a dark pile upon the floor... if the thing had even been his cousin. Reed bent by the mess - strips of flesh and fabric, no blood; but all in all, no indication as to what had truly happened. Was Potter gone? Had he been possessed by the Radiant King?

Or was it a disguise all along?

But if it had *been a disguise, why did the King wait and watch before attacking?*

He lifted his voice. "Aunty!"

Mors appeared before the final syllable, almost as though she had already been swooping down upon his apartment. "What is this, Reed?"

"I wish I knew. It looked like Potter."

Her bony head creaked as it shook. "No, he is attending to some business beyond the city. This was the Radiant King."

"Then you came to examine it?"

"The traces, yes," she said, pacing soundlessly now, her feet simply not relevant as far as his eyes were concerned. Not dissimilar to the exact specifics of her face. From the corner of his eye, he caught a flash from a streetlight as it burst into a shower of sparks.

Aunty was angry for once, it seemed. Luckily his own electronics were all switched off, at least.

"Can you follow them?"

"Such traces that remain do lead down of course... it is recuperating strength somewhere deeper, atop a tower."

"A deeper tower?"

"Yes." She straightened, and there was almost a sense of excitement – or at least new energy – to her generally static nature. "That is what I sensed before being shown a familiar blank slate."

That was one paradox too many for the moment. "But

the thing spoke as Potter. And it didn't attack right away. That doesn't make sense."

Her skull's frown was faint. "No, it does not." She turned to the doorway. A moment later, Potter appeared. "Did the Radiant King visit you?" she asked.

"No, was it here?"

"Yes. Impersonating you, it seems."

He strode over to examine the skin and robes, not bothering to greet Reed. "This is like me but it is certainly *not* me."

"Agreed," she said.

"So, the Radiant King is able to assume the identity of others?"

"Presumably."

"But at first, I didn't sense the burning sand or the worms like usual," Reed said. "Is it able to cloak that somehow?"

"Perhaps," Potter replied. "Another troubling revelation."

"It was able to sound and act a lot like you, Potter," Reed replied. "It even waited until I'd woken, letting me reach the kitchen before seeming to lose control and attack – which also doesn't make a lot of sense."

Potter turned to his mother. "This is becoming worse *far* quicker than we'd feared."

A nod.

"Wait, you expected something like this?" Reed asked.

"Not this precisely," she replied. "But all evidence gathered thus far suggests that, at a minimum, other forms may be taken. It can manipulate human flesh – clearly that includes into a shape not unlike Potter here. Perhaps it is, for now, a less sophisticated version of the doll Lina has created for you."

Reed nodded slowly. "Then what next?"

"Prepare," his aunt said. "The Radiant King will strike again within two days or fewer, to approximate your time."

"Will it be so long?"

"I believe this latest salvo has come at a significant cost."

"Which means this is the best chance to counter," Potter observed.

"I look forward to your help then," Reed replied.

The man did not answer.

"Max and Lina shall be sufficient, Reed," Mors said. "And I believe that not only Minerva but also Diana and Mars, may be sending someone along too."

Heartening, but it was hard to feel truly confident. "Will that be enough?"

"It must be."

"Why not make sure?"

She waved a bony hand. "Your implication is tiresome. You know the answer; we are not involved in the struggles here."

"This goes beyond the human world, clearly."

"Reed." Her voice had grown flatter.

"No! If the Radiant King is powerful enough to steal and hide Feronia's very hand, then this is a threat to you all," he said, raising his voice. "Why won't you admit that?"

"There are rules."

"They aren't my rules! Help us, gods be damned."

Mors actually sighed. "How many of your years now have we had this same conversation, again and again? Usually I might add, each time you face a challenge."

Reed stiffened. "Like my parents? Is that why you never found anything, your fucking rules?"

Potter stepped between Reed and Mors. "Enough." His very voice was a heavy hand upon Reed's chest, bearing down on him.

But Reed spat, "What are you going to do, cousin? Want to rough me up again, like when I was young? Well, I don't think you can, since apparently, *I'm* the only one who's allowed to take on the fucking job of saving you miserable pricks!"

Potter's shoulders trembled but he did not step any closer.

Mors only stared across at him with her dispassionate, hollow eye sockets. "Mark yourself and prepare, Reed."

Chapter 22.

Reed strode down the faded carpet of the Grand Towers hallway, heading for the silvery elevator. He had to meet Emma at the tattoo parlour before eight, but a familiar figure stepped off when the doors dinged open.

Constable Huggins.

The officer blinked, half raising a hand. "Wait, aren't you in—"

Reed offered a smile. "I'm out until they change their minds, I guess."

"I haven't heard about anything like this," he said with a frown.

"Duong keeping things from you now, is he?" Reed asked as they drew together. "Seems like him," he added, holding back a sneer at himself. It was a cruel thing to play upon Huggins' situation, but going back to jail was definitely not an option.

"Well..."

"Look, maybe he isn't." Reed shrugged. "But if you're here to see me I'm on my way out. Happy to reschedule."

"No, actually," the man said. "I'll leave my request on hold… for now," he said, still frowning. "I'm actually investigating something else, it's a little strange."

"In the building?"

He nodded. "The bottom floors have a strange hole in them, like someone drilled up from the ground. Which they did, but we can't figure out why. The hole's only got the circumference of a flagpole but it's extremely neat."

Reed hesitated. Had he actually checked his own bedroom floor? "When did that happen?"

"Last night. I'm still taking statements, waiting for the forensics team to arrive."

"I didn't notice anything but I'd love to hear about whatever you find," he said.

"Of course. Are you heading out for a meal or…?"

"Getting a tattoo, actually – *Anderson Tattoo and Piercing*, if you want to check up on me."

"Oh?"

"Yep. My first one. I'll let you know how much it hurts."

"Well, good luck."

Reed thanked him and hopped onto the elevator, riding down in silence, tapping one foot.

And once he'd jogged through the foyer to rush from the building and into the car park, he homed in on his rental then leapt into the driver's seat. A nervous energy was building, and running into the law had only ramped it up. "Let's go," he said as he backed out, gripping the wheel hard, so hard that he didn't even jump when Max appeared in the back seat.

"Off to get 'inked' then?" his cousin asked.

"I'm meeting Emma there."

"Mind if I tag along?"

"Only if you don't talk when we're inside."

"Hmmm."

Reed frowned at the long press of cars and trams. But if there was an unbeatable benefit when it came to city-living that he could trade off against the traffic, it was the service. *Everything* was open at pretty much all hours, even tattoo parlours. "So, who else is coming with us?"

"Down the rabbit hole? We three, of course. Adrina is scouting the other sites for now, but Mars is sending along Diego. I don't know if you've met him?"

"I don't think so. Isn't he the one who bit the head off Neptune's pet shark?"

"Yes, but it was an accident."

"Accident?"

Max leant forward. "Well, there was a lot going on at the time, you see. We were having a party for Conditor and everyone was a little drunk and we'd tricked him into taking a swim but he was covered in –"

"Wait, I don't think I need all the details."

He pouted. "Fine. Well, Diego can be a lot of fun, actually."

"So long as he's strong, I guess," Reed replied.

"Absolutely. Great with any weapon; you might have seen him with the axes when we dealt with the cultists?"

"Not that I remember."

"No matter." Max leant back with a sigh. "Are you sure you don't want to ask *why* Diego ate half a shark?"

"I hadn't planned to."

"Fine. I'll just tell you later then. Or better yet, let him tell the tale. Or face." Max paused, as though waiting.

"What is it?"

"Tell me you heard that joke."

He shook his head. "Max, is there a point to this?"

"Yes. Same as last time – you seem especially tense and I want to take the edge off."

Reed swerved as a pedestrian stepped out from the curb, face buried in a sandwich and staring down at their phone. His grip caused the wheel to squeak. "Yeah, I am."

"I heard you got a little upset with Potter and Mother."

"You have a flair for understatement, you know that?"

"Well?"

"Sounds like you have something to say."

"Maybe. I just want you to remember that whatever the rules Mother has to abide by, Lina and I will still help you. You're family, Reed – even if the others sometimes forget it."

Reed glanced in the mirror. Max appeared far more earnest than usual. "Thanks. That's nice to hear, actually."

"Atta boy."

"We're still in trouble, you know," Reed said as he came to a halt before a red light. The sky was overcast, casting the glassy buildings and cars and umbrellas in a dull light. "The Radiant King isn't getting weaker and we don't really know where it is, let alone how to stop it. If we do find that thing down there and the five of us aren't enough, what then?"

"Presumably the Gods themselves will step in."

"And that's exactly what pisses me off. If things are truly in the balance, why gamble on us? They could take action together right now."

"You know why – the rules."

"That's bullshit."

"To you, yes. And maybe even to me and the other younglings to some extent, but maybe you're forgetting something obvious, Reed. This world isn't *that* important to them – they can always make another." Max offered what seemed like a sad shrug. "There have been times where there was no planet like this, no humans like you wandering around killing and torturing each other."

Reed said nothing at first. *Max is right, though.* "That's not all we do."

"Fine. But that wasn't my point."

"Yeah, I know," he said. "Look, understanding *why* they act that way doesn't mean I'm comforted. I think it just makes me want to fight even more."

"Very noble of you, cousin."

"I guess I think humans deserve at least a little more time to get things right," he said as he approached the turn, this street one full of exposed brick cafe-style shops, but also the chrome and leather of *Anderson Tattoo and Piecing.*

And, blissfully, there was a park not too far from the front door, where Emma stood before the shop. She wore a dark green coat and had one hand on her hip.

"Then let's put a stop to this thing, then," Max said.

"Right."

Chapter 23.

Tattoo now complete, Reed sat by the window of a somewhat steamy cafe Max and Lina had created. He ran a finger over the raised, ink-filled skin upon his upper arm, the plastic wrap covering it for now. It really was an elegant symbol. Emma sat beside him but she didn't check her wrist, seeming perhaps a little more blasé about it. *And why not? It's her third or fourth.*

"It's ready," Max called from the kitchen.

While the room bore some aspects of a typical Melbourne cafe, with the exposed rafters and beautiful silver bar, it didn't actually reside in the city. For one, the place was empty save for Reed and the others, and two, Max and Lina had always claimed to actually own it.

The final clue was the vista beyond the windows; a hothouse with garland-like flourishes on the steel sculptures of animals, half-lost to a riot of green and pink plants. Glimpses of deep blue ferns were visible too, misty rain fading beneath a high sun.

Reed had visited several times before, though it was

usually too humid to stay for a long while. Somehow, the place was meant to evoke the Fringe but not actually harm humans who might have needed to visit.

There were other oddities; chiefly the food, since while each bite tasted wonderful, it somehow left him hungrier than when he began. Worse, today's meal had a Last Supper feeling about it which he didn't care for.

But his attention mostly fell upon Diego.

A handsome fellow – all the Gods' children seemed to be good-looking in one way or another – he bore a vague 1930s movie star look, with his pencil-thin moustache. But the man was bulkier, like a body-builder and his short hair was jet black, contrasted by the white of his wide smile.

He leant upon the table, bracers of steel upon his wrists. His breastplate had been carved with crossed blades before a shield, but seemed as much a part of him as his skin. Mighty twin axes rested nearby, the handles wrapped in black.

"You should have let me help," Diego said, his voice booming but sincere.

"No trouble," Lina said as she joined Max in collecting the now empty plates, then returning with drinks of vivid blue. Half of the meal was actual food but the rest, which had been offered to the gods' children, seemed almost ritualistic.

Reed accepted his drink with a smile. "This looks great."

"How sweet you are," Lina replied. "But it's from Apollo, not me."

"That's welcome," Reed said as he drank, the revitalising liquid straightening him in his chair, the strength that followed equally pleasant. *Maybe we have a good chance after all.*

"So, would you like to discuss our possible deaths before

or after we finish our drinks?" Lina asked.

"You're a funny girl, Lina," Max said with a sigh.

"I'd prefer the word 'practical' to be honest."

Diego nodded. "Let's get it – and the bitter taste it'll bring – out of the way, shall we? Then we can relax with our mostly human brethren in peace."

"Agreed," Lina said.

"It's certainly fine with me," Emma added her voice, but she glanced down at her own glass. "This will help me, somehow?"

Reed grinned. "It will."

"Okay." She looked around the table, her expression calm and commanding. "Shall I begin then?"

Nods.

"All right." She spread her hands upon the table. "We all know that the Radiant King manifests as something human-like, and that shape is in turn directed by the thing's true form – which is our true target. We can deal with dozens of shells and never get close to the real problem."

"Right," Max nodded.

"To stand before either shell or the true King, I believe that Minerva has guided me to the truth in our tattoos. We shouldn't be sealed in stone as Max and Lina had been. From Mors, we know that there is a tower beneath the city that we must reach, but we do not know what we will find there."

"Maybe it won't be so different to the outside," Reed said, gesturing beyond the glass. "After all, the Radiant King did take Feronia's hand."

"No assumptions, though."

He smiled. "Agreed."

"Next is the time limit. Again, Mors believes we have about a day and a half before the Radiant King can seek the world above ground again. That might not mean much, depending on where we end up down there."

"Don't you mean, 'when' we end up down there?" Max asked, attempting to hold back a grin.

"You hate us, don't you?" Lina asked.

"Meaning?"

"You think those poor jokes are actually good but they aren't, that's the first problem. But worse than that, I think you only say them to make us die inside a little each time."

"Can we do that? Die inside, I mean. Or die at all, do you think?"

"Max, please," Reed said with a frown.

He raised both hands.

Diego hid a smile behind his own arm, before asking Emma a question. "It sounds like we have a few things in order but what did you and your Mistress discover about the Radiant King, the true identity?"

"Little, I fear."

"Then we still face the unknown, unsure of whether we are up to the challenge, I see."

"Do you wish to back down, Diego?" Max asked.

"Not at all. Are we not the five most important beings upon the earth this very moment? I could hardly miss this."

"What was the little you found, Emma?" Reed asked.

"Well... we know it is old. Perhaps pre-dating Lord Jupiter. We know the hand used the Book of Hours to leave this realm and that the Radiant King is learning English, perhaps slowly. It seems to collect people and possibly things. Reed witnessed it take a human and a werewolf. The

King has impersonated one of Death's children too, in what seemed to be an attempt to take Reed himself."

"And all of that implies something, right?" Max asked.

"I believe so. Aside from more evidence of its vast age, the King seems to *want* someone to find it, wherever it may be. And it is possible that the someone is Reed."

Diego nodded slowly. "Hmmm."

Reed sat back in his chair, a chill falling over him and the effects of Apollo's drink fading – at least, the confidence it had given him. "You think that taking Phillip was more of a taunt? That it wants *me* to follow, knowing I need Phillip as a witness?"

"Yes."

"And when I didn't immediately do so, it tried to take me via the Potter disguise?"

"I think that's very possible, and if we consider what we're about to do, it's certainly working. You're on your way to its lair."

"It is... but that's an assumption too far, isn't it? It may just want *any* of Death's children; they've been targets before."

"True, but there is also the smell of burning sand and the feeling of worms and paper to consider."

"Like your parents," Lina said, nodding slowly.

"Maybe."

"We have heard you well," Diego said. "But are you suggesting that Reed's mother and father are part of this?"

"No." Emma shook her head. "I think it's far more likely that whatever took *them* may now want Reed too." She met his gaze. "I've been wondering about this for a while... but I didn't want to bring it up. I'm a little surprised you hadn't thought of it."

Was it possible? *Whether it's likely or only* possible... *I've suddenly got another reason to go down there.* "I've had a bit on my mind," he mumbled. Then he stood and began to pace the room.

"Reed?"

"Just need a minute." He glanced over his shoulder to the table. There was more to the Radiant King, surely. "What about the worms and paper? That caught your attention, remember?"

She nodded. "It did. I went digging and I found something after all. It's not exactly the same, but it's supposedly a Mesopotamia myth, except certain things don't match."

"Let's hear it, anyway."

"Right. Tell me if you all agree. A creature walks the night, feet soundless on sand, and when it nears, the people speak of tasting freshly turned earth. If they keep their doors and windows closed it does not trouble them but for any fool who opens their home, or cannot find shelter, they will face a creeping thing whose skin rustles against its own skin to the tune of soft leaves rustling."

Reed straightened. "They *could* be related... worms are obviously associated with the earth."

"And the sound of leaves becoming the sense of paper?" Lina suggested.

"Then this thing has changed, if it is so?" Diego asked.

"Perhaps."

"Was there any mention of how to banish the thing?"

Emma sighed. "People of the villages in the myth would sing but it was not recorded what song, nor any of the words. One boy was said to drive it away via water blessed by a healer but that's too vague, I think."

Reed lifted the Sonorous free very carefully, a hand upon the clapper. "It didn't like this, when I faced it underground."

Diego chuckled. "Too bad we can't all carry bells; maybe we could make half a tune."

"Maybe we can, actually," Max said, glancing to Lina.

"Are you sure?" Reed asked.

Diego slapped the table, rattling plates. "If so, isn't it worth a shot?"

"Of course," Lina replied. "But the bells Reed has in mind are used for Banishing, remember? Things that come from the Fringe or beyond tend to get sent home from this plane."

"Even the children of Death?"

"If we're under duress, yes," she replied. "It's especially hard to resist the Sonorous' call, since it is one of the most powerful chimes, second only to the Great Bell of Dhammazedi – but humans haven't uncovered that yet. Likely, the Sonorous would also work on you."

"I see."

Max nodded. "I still think it would be worth at least having Emma carry one too. And maybe me," he said. "As a last resort, even though it would send me from the tower, I think we should be prepared."

Reed returned to the table. "But what if we try it and you are Banished? What if all of you are sent beyond the Fringe – Emma and I would be left to face the Radiant King alone."

A pause from Max. "If we see the Sonorous has an impact then we will consider it. If not, yours is a valid concern."

"So, what now?" Lina asked.

"It seems there is nothing else we can plan for," Diego said. "We have our ward, we will soon have some chimes and we have an approximate location. Perhaps there is now naught but the actual task before us?"

"So it would seem," Reed said softly.

Chapter 24.

Reed peered through the rip in the Fringe, where it lurked at the bottom of a plunging hole they'd followed beneath the city.

The Radiant King had made the opening but Reed knew that another one would lie beyond, and that this would lead to the creature's hiding place – a tower. And while Max, and Lina, and especially Diego, had offered to pass through first, he'd refused. *I want to be the one.*

Bravery, stupidity or something else?

Why not all three?

"So, if there's a tower beyond a second tear that I'm sure is just beneath us here, I think there's going to be a pretty rough moment of vertigo," Reed said.

"We'll be fine," Max replied. "Up and down don't mean quite the same thing to us."

"I'm sure Emma will be thrilled to hear that."

"Oh."

She smiled. "I'm not great with heights, you see."

"Well, we'll try to ease the passage somehow," Max said.

Reed gripped the edges of the opening and paused. "Someone bring one of the gods if something happens."

"We will," Diego said.

"Thanks."

Reed dropped down – and the world tilted. Darkness and light alike both swept up from beneath him, yet somehow the light was *already above him*. He stumbled, falling into an ungainly crouch as the flip in whatever gravity existed here pushed and pulled at him at the same time.

And then his vision cleared and the pressure eased, and he could stand. His stomach twisted inside but he didn't need to throw up at least.

Within the tower things were... different.

Reed stood in a circular chamber bearing a spiral staircase, with regular landings adorned by greenery. Blazing light from high above lit unusual walls – they appeared as moulded bodies with blank faces, most in kneeling rows. They did not push too far out from the wall, yet no human sculptor could have made them. Nor were they actual humans either, since no hint of departed souls remained.

A few figures were standing, or appeared half in flight; almost like leaping ballerinas, as though whoever had made the tower had grown bored with the pattern... *All work and no play makes jack a dull boy*. Reed shared a glance with Emma, who was shaking her head. "This doesn't feel right."

"Agreed, but how so for you?" Max asked.

"It's not any more or less disturbing than I'd have imagined, I suppose, but it's very conventional. Walls, stairs, a tower... why would such a powerful being need to create such a thing?"

Max nodded slowly. "Indeed, my dear."

"We must climb it no matter what, of course," Diego said.

"Right." Lina skipped toward the foot of the stair, and started up. "The steps are interesting. They all look like smeared irises."

Reed frowned down at the streaks of colour – blue, green and golden brown running together. At times it was an ugly mess, and other times it was beautiful. Why had the Radiant King made such a place? Emma's question suggested that the king required or *wanted* human servants, surely?

And if that were so, did it mean that the king was, in some small ways at least, following the rules?

Upon the first landing Reed found more kneeling shapes, this time supporting a guard rail. Potted plants grew upon it, though of course the pots were not in any way normal. Instead, each seemed to be trying to replicate rib cages... only some were closer to webs.

And then the plants themselves: the root system and soil remained visible, pulsing slightly as the greenery grew, literally as he watched the leaves grew longer, then withered down. But before each leaf faded from its brown to full grey, a pale yellow thread appeared to bounce back and the leaf became green once more.

"No sign that Feronia's hand might have been here at all," Max said.

Lina snorted as she continued up.

Max leapt after her with a grin. "Come on! I passed over at least six bad puns before settling on that juicy bit of sarcasm. Do you want to–?"

"No."

Reed hung back a little with Emma as the others continued the long climb. "How are you going so far?"

"I'd love a hand rail all the way up, but if I can keep the inside lane I'll be fine."

He shifted a little and she took the side of the stairway closer to the wall, striding up confidently enough. Reed kept pace, using his body to hopefully shield at least the *sense* of the drop beside him. *Best you don't make that too obvious, assuming it's even helpful.*

On they climbed.

The tower stretched up; more human-moulded walls, more landings with their immortal-seeming plants and still there seemed no end in sight. Whenever he craned his neck it was just the same stretching stair topped by brightness.

"Is this some sort of loop?" Reed called ahead as Max, Lina and Diego reached another landing.

"No, but I agree that we don't seem to be making a lot of progress."

"Hmmm." Lina moved to one of the plants and gave it a nudge.

It tumbled over the rail and fell like a stone – or, like heavy soil contained in a spidery ribcage of bone-that-might-not-have-been-bone. It plummeted down and after thirty seconds or so, a faint shattering echoed up.

Grinding echoed from one of the walls on the landing.

"Be ready for something," Reed said.

"That's nice and specific," Max replied, but he had braced himself a little. Diego stood beside him, grinning with both axes ready.

But when a section of wall slid open to reveal a dark opening, there was no beast or raging Radiant King, but instead, a small bald man dressed in black robes stepped through. He raised a hand in greeting. "We have guests, I see."

His voice came from an inhumanly wide mouth, but other than that oddity, he was relatively normal.

Max frowned. "Who are you, if we might ask?"

"Something of a Gatekeeper, if you like."

"I don't know yet."

"Know what?"

"Whether I like what you just said."

The bald man seemed to chew upon his lip in confusion, a glimpse of sharp teeth visible. "But... you understand what I said?"

"We do, yes."

He smiled now, and Reed almost flinched. The fellow had *a lot* of teeth and they were indeed all quite sharp. *Like a goddamn mouthful of piranhas.* "Wonderful. I believe you have all been deemed suitable too."

"Thank you," Lina said.

The Gatekeeper nodded. "If you follow me a moment, I will take you to the outskirts but I cannot accompany you further."

"The outskirts of what?" Reed asked.

The Gatekeeper smiled again, showing more teeth. "It's not far, Mr Lavender."

Chapter 25.

The outskirts were precisely what Reed expected – and also not at all what he'd imagined.

Beyond where the short Gatekeeper stood within the wall's shadow, arm extended, waited fields of gently swaying grass. A smooth, sealed road complete with fencing and a signpost led toward a single home upon a slight crest. Further on came the sense of a town – perhaps it was a hint of some haze, like autumn home-fires.

It was a mild enough day in the place the Radiant King had chosen, but the sun did appear watery. And the signpost was not precisely using numbers and words, the symbols were just 'off' enough to seem like half-educated errors. Even the fences bore a rigidly similar swirl to the wood grain.

"You need only to travel that road to find His Majesty," the Gatekeeper said.

"A shame it isn't yellow," Max murmured.

Again, the Gatekeeper did not seem equipped to understand the joke, eventually settling on a smile. "I see."

"So, the Radiant King is waiting for us?" Emma asked.

"Most keenly for Mr Lavender, yes, but you will all be welcomed here."

Reed paused. "Especially me?"

"And what do you mean by 'welcomed' exactly?" Lina added.

"His Majesty will answer all questions, of course," he said. "While the daylight lingers, it would be best if you could make a start. There are still more than a few accidents running around out there, is all."

"Accidents?"

The Gatekeeper nodded as the wall began to slide closed. "Indeed."

"Wait!" Reed leapt for the opening, but it was already sealed. He thumped upon the moulded surface but the Gatekeeper did not answer. Reed groaned as he turned. "Any ideas of what he meant? Can you feel anything?"

Max and Lina both nodded, as did Diego.

"Because all I sense is a wall of the same dark *wrongness* from this place," Reed continued. "And that's probably not the 'accidents' he mentioned."

"I'd say the Radiant King's presence is such that it will conceal anything additional until it's pretty close," Max said.

"Let's get moving then," Reed said with a nod.

Once again his cousins took the lead, Diego at the point of their little wedge, leaving Reed to walk beside Emma.

She was checking on the muffled clapper of her bell, the Adagio, which Aunty had dropped off before their climb. "I can't help wondering, is this going to be enough?

Will it even work here?" she asked when she finished.

"No way to test it without the risk of banishing the others, sadly."

"Exactly." She sighed. "Your bell and this one, my Words and the others... how many did it take to stop Feronia?"

"Best not to dwell on that too much."

"You've asked your Aunty similar questions, Reed."

"I have."

"And how did you like not receiving a straight answer?"

Reed raised a hand. "Right, sorry. I should know better because I've certainly never received an answer I liked. But we do have the Bells and my cousins aren't exactly slouches." He pulled his handgun from the bag he'd carried all the way up the damn tower. "And if there are humans down here... up here, wherever we are... or if the King himself has a human part, then I have this too."

"But we did spend a little bit of time in the Fringe, will that still function?"

"I hope so, just in case," he said. "I even painted Aunty's mark on the bullets."

The home had drawn near; it was a thatched cottage. The walls were even white-washed and a small window-box housed bright flowers. But just like the rest of the place above the tower, some things were askew: the petals were square for one, and when he approached the dusty window, brush-strokes became visible on the flowers.

He reached out to touch them – and it was not the waxy feel of fake plants, it seemed real enough but still, it had clearly been painted. It also seemed to be surviving the thick paint.

"This place is empty," Max called from the front, where

Diego stood guard upon the road.

Reed joined his cousin. Inside the home lay nothing but dirt.

No rooms, no walls, no furniture – nothing at all that suggested it had been created to house actual people.

"Let's see what else is waiting for us, then," Reed said.

He led them along the road at a stride, the fields now bordered by woods. Some trees grew far closer to the road and even in between further empty homes, these all similar but growing larger. A few even featured walls to denote rooms.

The road, too, had switched to an intricate cobblestone pattern and it led to a roundabout that circled a fountain complete with neat garden beds. In the centre of the dry fountain was something like Michelago's David, only the face had melted and the arms and hands were truly out of proportion. And nor did he stand with sling in hand; instead David held a trail of serpents.

"It's like he jammed part of Cellini's sculpture into the *David*," Emma said.

"Odd," Reed replied. An understatement that would have made Max proud. *Maybe this place is getting to me; I'm feeling a little numb.*

"But it doesn't speak of incompetence, I don't think," Lina noted as she gazed instead at the surrounding buildings, half of which were shops with large glass fronts. Though most were empty, a few actually had furniture and even electrical items within.

"No?" Emma asked. "Do you mean more like... honest mistakes? Or maybe playfulness?"

"Right. It's almost as though he is more powerful but

less comfortable with humanity than we assumed."

"Are you saying you think it's not one of the usual Gods?" Reed asked.

"I think so, especially after what Emma brought us."

Diego swung one of his blades, leaving it pointing at the nearest shop. "Would it be prudent to take a quick look within, to make sure there are no surprises before we move on then?"

"Right," Max agreed. "Stay in pairs, I think."

"There's obviously five of us, Max," Reed said as he and Emma joined Diego.

"How silly of me, yes."

In the shop, they found grey and white kitchen electronics *and* crockery with displays of silverware in glass cabinets. A logical collection, just not arranged so. But when Reed took a square plate of a brilliant blue and held it up before one of the microwaves, it was clear one had not been designed with the other in mind.

Nor would any plate in the store fit the microwave.

And more, the brand name was missing a vowel. He glanced at Emma, who held a 'spork' – yet one of such fine, ornate silver that it had to be ornamental. "This entire place feels like a mistake, doesn't it?" she asked.

Reed nodded.

Chapter 26.

The next two 'towns' were similar.

So far, they'd found two more places full of failed proportions and branding, but with each one improvements had been made. Sometimes it was just the writing, mostly English, but in other buildings it was only singular successes – a functioning chimney, a working oven or a lounge suite arranged before a television.

Sometimes the colours were off, or the patterns upon shirts too rigid or garish but they did at least appear human-sized. Back in the second town, Reed remembered a pair of underpants that could have doubled as a tourniquet and which had been paired with a fairly regular-sized pair of socks.

"Most things are getting better," Reed said as they left the latest of the King's empty hamlets.

"No more roads that terminate in grass," Emma replied.

"Or the tree line."

From ahead, Diego gave a shout. "Be ready!"

Reed pulled the Sonorous free, gripping the clapper as

he straightened. Something was rustling the trees beyond the fence of the nearest backyard.

Emma had lifted her gloved hands, the hint of silver thread gleaming. Supposedly woven with two strands of Minerva's hair, with the gloves Emma could sketch letters in the air and send the commands forth – it was like a superhero movie. Reed had only ever seen them once before. "You didn't mention that you'd borrowed those," he said, glancing back to the trees.

"I didn't really want the others to see them until we were in here," she replied.

"Why not?"

"In case they let it slip; you know what it's like with the Children, they all know what the others know *very* quickly."

"You mean you just took them? Minerva will have you flayed, won't she?"

Emma grinned, though it seemed a little tense. "Not if we succeed."

A stout figure burst from the trees.

The thing was no bigger than a tiger or lion but its skin was a flinty grey. Yet a vague luminescence was *trapped* beneath the surface. It charged in an unusual gait, using oversized forearms to propel itself at the fence.

A spray of wood and earth followed.

When it neared, the thing's features became clear. It possessed a flat, eyeless face with a jutting lower jaw, only there were no teeth, rather a sharp, bone-like ridge.

Despite this it had no trouble sensing them and it picked up its pace, a shoulder crashing through the edge of the house.

"Scatter," Max called. "It cannot turn quickly."

Reed circled away as Emma stalked in the opposite direction, but the thing seemed to have chosen a target – Diego, who did not move. Instead, he braced himself and raised both axes.

"Let me draw it!" he cried.

Reed swapped the Sonorous for his gun as a streak of light flashed by. It burnt the very air as it moved. Emma had sent a rune forth; even now she was sketching another before her, silvery lines trailing her hands. The first struck the side of the creature, which stumbled but once, before continuing to bear down on Diego with remaining momentum.

He swung both axes down in an overhand blow.

A mighty thud echoed in the emptiness. Dust and chipped stone flew out in a circle, the force of the blow so great.

The thing collapsed.

Diego grunted as he wrenched at his axes, but both seemed stuck fast. Reed approached, gun held ready, but the thing wasn't moving. When he drew close enough, joined by the others, he saw that the creature *did* have eyes, but they were thin, placed low and near the mouth. Not too different from a turtle, perhaps.

"What is it?" he asked.

The body stirred and movement flashed.

Diego roared as he fell back, clutching his arm. Reed flinched away, but he'd been too slow if he'd been the target – his eyes hadn't registered anything beyond a vague blur... but now he could see, it was a swaying serpent that wore a Radiant Crown.

The snake had risen from the body of the 'accident',

slender but like lightning.

Greetings all. The voice that issued forth was not sibilant, but firm, commanding. *I have prepared a larger welcoming party for you and I am most interested to see how you fare.*

And then the serpent receded back into the body, leaving behind a hint of burning sand.

Lina circled the corpse to check on Diego. "Your arm is already turning grey."

He nodded where he'd wrapped a large hand around his forearm, as if to stem the flow of grey that spread across his limb toward his hand. *Similar enough to what happened to Max and Lina to be a sign of real trouble.* The big man glanced up at her. "I can certainly slow it but I believe I'll need a little more brute strength to fight off the poison. I need a little extra room, if you could."

Lina skipped back.

Diego let go of his arm, then closed his eyes to smash both palms together with a grunt.

He clenched his hands then, and dark ochre spread, swiftly overcoming the grey. It ran further along his skin and body. At the same time, Diego grew. His muscled torso expanded until he became Hulk-like and a dark mane burst free from his head. Next, his face elongated to that of a bull, dark eyes blazing. Horns of curled gold sprouted forth too, and he snorted before stooping to retrieve his weapons.

Yet he was not done, for these too he clanged together, moulding them into a single, double-headed great axe.

"You're a minotaur?" Emma asked.

"Certainly I can be," he replied, and his voice had grown deeper. "It seemed the best way to deal with the poison and blessedly, I am stronger."

Reed couldn't prevent a smile. "I'm definitely impressed."

"It warms my heart to hear it."

"If you're all finished admiring our bullish friend, I think this is worth seeing," Max announced from nearby.

He knelt before the Accident, pointing. His eyes were entirely black where he waited. Reed nearly nodded to himself, no doubt Max and Lina had been trying to decompose or separate the creature the whole time; it already seemed smaller.

But where his cousin pointed lay the truly unusual part – twin wedges rested in the thing's head, and each cut revealed tightly bundled pages. Each page was nearly buried in words. As if a book had been cut almost in half...

"What are these creatures?" Reed asked.

Emma was already studying it, lips pursed.

But she had no answer.

When she stepped closer he frowned. "Are you sure the Radiant King can't strike again? The poison looks like its bile," Reed said. "And maybe Emma's helped Diego, but we don't know how well."

"In time we will know, as I must be that test," Diego said.

Emma had taken a few steps around the Accident's body now. "The Gatekeeper's description was accurate enough. From what I can tell, some words here relate to the animal kingdom."

"Then what was this meant to be?" Lina asked. "A gorilla or a rhino... a turtle? I'm seeing a little of everything here."

Footsteps approached from the road.

A single figure strolled toward them, dressed in jeans and white shirt, shotgun slung over one shoulder. Upon the shirt rested what could have been a sheriff's badge, gleaming in the light, but the man's face was still too distant to recognise.

"You're all trespassing, I'm sorry to say," a familiar voice announced.

Chapter 27.

Phillip the hit-man.

His balding head was hidden beneath a faded red baseball cap, but his dark brows were still set in the frown Reed remembered from the man's house, before Patrick had snapped the assassin's collar bone.

Phillip seemed well enough now...in a way; his skin bore the same grey with slight luminescence of the Accident. It wasn't the only change, considering the sheriff's badge, and while it bore no particular name, the shotgun seemed accurate enough. A rather grotesque inversion of the truth.

The Radiant King's sheriff stopped half a dozen steps away, and from behind him a line of Accidents appeared – all far smaller than the corpse nearby, but they numbered in the dozens. "Now, there are penalties for what you've all done folks, but I have an offer that you should hear first."

Reed stepped forward, almost shaking his head at the parodical nature of the scene. "You are not Phillip, are you? You're the Radiant King."

He paused. "No. It is more that 'we' are the Radiant

King now, Mr Lavender."

"Then you've been duped, Phillip."

"I disagree."

"Where is Patrick?"

The fake sheriff shrugged. "Ran off when I was being improved."

Reed still held his own gun but would a bullet even work? If it didn't do much other than slow the man down, then that'd give everyone else time if nothing else. Hopefully Max and Lina were already working on the Accidents. But it was good news about Patrick, at least. "Then you can finally tell me the truth. No more bullshit, Phillip. Did you kill Elise?"

A nod. "You knew that, already."

Reed spoke through a clenched jaw. "Because Robert Dunstall ordered you to, and because she wasn't working out when it came to trafficking product? Or because of the Shining Leaves?"

"It had nothing to do with the cult; she couldn't handle the business side of things."

"She was just a kid," Reed snapped. Gaining confirmation of something he'd long sought hadn't granted much satisfaction.

"Old enough to know right from wrong, I'd have thought," Phillip replied. "But I think that's enough about the past. His Majesty would like me to tell you that he sees potential in all of you. You can each be of use here, if you submit yourself to him."

"I don't think so," Max said as he joined Reed. "And you have to know we're here to stop all of this."

"Well, that's what He expected, but I'm allowed to deal with you all if it comes to that – all accept Mr Lavender."

"Why?" Reed demanded.

Phillip's mouth did not move, but still the words rang in Reed's mind. *All work and no play makes Jack a dull boy.*

The Accidents charged in a wave of grey.

Diego leapt into them, great axe flashing. Smaller grey bodies were flung across the road, some crashing into the trees and others through the walls of nearby homes, but enough passed the minotaur that Max and Lina had to stop them – simply by staring at each Accident, twin sets of black eyes Reaping the things.

Phillip had darted forth, circling away from Diego. He raised his shotgun but Emma had already cast a glimmering rune to snap around the barrel. And though he still pulled the trigger, the burst and flash was slow – the spray of pellets growing in a dull web.

And there it hung in the air, moving at a crawl.

Emma didn't even flinch.

Reed fired his own gun. The bullet tore through Phillip's shoulder, driving him back half a step. No blood blossomed.

He hurled the gun aside and charged around the slowly spreading bullets. Emma gave ground but Reed leapt after Phillip, skeletal hands outstretched. He caught the hit-man around the waist and together they crashed to the ground, fighting for the upper hand – because while Reed's grip was stronger than a normal human, there was no way 'in' to Phillip now.

And the false sheriff was stronger than he ought to have been.

The man was smiling. "You certainly fell for that ploy, Mr Lavender."

Reed ground his teeth, squeezing the man's wrist. "Did I?"

"I need just a moment now and we can leave your friends to their toil."

Phillip's eyes began to darken as tines pushed through his granite-like skin of his forehead, tips blackened. Reed pulled back... but Phillip was no longer moving; he may not have even been *Phillip* anymore.

The man's skin had swiftly grown icy.

"Reed, get back!" Emma shouted. She was sketching in the air still, and it seemed the word was *ghiaccio*, one of her favourites; 'freeze' in Italian.

Reed wrenched himself free, breathing hard.

Phillips eyes were still moving, though his body did seem set in place, even if no ice had formed.

You have failed.

The Radiant King's voice rang clearly in Reed's mind but the words did not seem to be directed his way... they were for Phillip.

The 'improved' hit-man cried out. "Majesty!"

Worry not, for in your return to me you are absolved.

And then Phillip began to shudder and shrink, growing thinner until he was no more than a grey puddle lurking within his shirt and jeans. When a breeze came, pieces of the man twisted up to float away, spinning across the road.

"That wasn't too difficult, I suppose," Max said as he approached. Diego towered behind him and Lina, and in turn, dozens of Accidents lay mute and still.

"But what's next?" Reed muttered. "The thing wants me."

"Then we face it and stop it," Lina replied.

You may of course attempt such a thing. The Radiant King

was nowhere in sight but it was obviously able to see them easily enough. *I rejoice, for in your own eventual failure I will attain ever stronger servants. You are each* quite *interesting.*

"Why not come and take us now, then?" Reed shouted back.

I await you upon my throne.

And then nothing more. Reed had to shake his head. The creature really did consider everything a damn game. He glanced at his friends. No-one seemed especially thrilled, but his anger was building beyond any fear. "I'm getting pretty fucking fed up with being jerked around, aren't you?"

Chapter 28.

Once again, Reed found himself travelling away from yet another empty town. No people, no animals, just buildings that were nearly fully functional; logos correct, words upon the menus and signs accurate now.

And a first so far – motorbikes, cars and trucks.

He glanced in the rear-view mirror as he pushed his foot down a little harder, engine growling in response. The immaculately clean ute thumped across a dip in the tarmac. In the tray, Diego was bounced around but did not complain.

"Where does the fuel come from, that's what I want to know," Max said from the passenger seat. Lina rolled her eyes in the backseat, and Emma did not appear to be listening, eyes upon the rows of fields that rolled by, some now bearing windmills.

"You always had an eye for the important details, Max," Lina said.

"I think it's valid. Am I supposed to believe that the Radiant King bothered to raid an oil refinery to fill up all these cars that no-one is using?"

"Maybe he *made* one," Reed said, hands firm on the steering wheel. "Like the rest of this strange place."

"That's certainly possible. We don't know anything about the limits here."

"You can't sense anything?"

"No. He's too strong. It's like he dampens everything. I can't tell if there's a forest or a painted wall beyond that stand of trees."

"Maybe we should try scouting ahead again," Lina suggested.

"Too risky," Reed replied.

"Is that so? *You* wouldn't be doing it, remember."

"I don't want to have to worry about you."

"Touching, but it might be the best choice. We've already been driving for... ah, I think an hour, right? And if I scout it's basically instant."

Reed frowned at her in the mirror. "I still don't like it."

"Neither do I," Emma said. "I think the king would be pleased if we split up. Easier for him to pick us off."

"Assuming he can't do that any time he pleases?" Max asked.

"I know, but surely he *can't* just take us all at once, otherwise he would have done it already," Emma replied.

Lina was nodding. "That's likely. But we're still heading into the unknown at... 116 kilometres an hour now."

Reed eased off the pedal a little. "I do want you to try your usual methods of moving about, you know."

"Oh?"

"Yeah. If this goes badly, I want you to take Emma out of here. Instantly, the way you travel."

"That would not be pleasant for Emma, Reed. She'd

sleep for a day afterwards, and some people don't actually wake up the same."

"Look, I know all that but I don't like this. We're being forced to spring a trap, it's risky."

"Yes, well maybe Emma *didn't* know the risks," Lina replied.

"Fine."

Lina didn't answer, but Emma leant forward and put a hand on his shoulder. "Cool it, Reed. And by the way, I don't agree to any of that. We're doing this together."

"That sounds like 'last words' to me."

"I'm planning on getting through this," she said, as she squeezed his shoulder. "I have plants to water."

The gesture drew his attention to all the tension he'd stored in his muscles, but her ridiculous claim was enough to make him smile. "No other plans? Just plants?"

"For now."

Reed ran a hand through his hair. "All right, I get it. And sorry, Lina. I'm still pissed off, I guess."

"It's no problem," she said. "That was nothing. I still remember that tantrum you threw back in Eden."

"Tantrum?"

Max was smiling. "Ah, yes, at the whale museum. That *was* funny, you know."

Reed glared at his cousin. "I could have been crushed."

"Possibly."

Emma leant forward to point ahead. "I think we're close."

Through the windscreen Reed saw the road widen to four lanes, like a misplaced freeway that led to a low stone wall. But the wall opened up to what seemed to be an amphitheatre where vehicles had been arranged in a circle.

The cars, jeeps and trucks blocked whatever they faced.

But from the growing sense of dry paper pressing against his skin, and the slimy taste of worms, Reed did not have to guess.

Roll up, roll up.

He frowned at the voice and eased the brake on. Even the 'non-sound' of the Radiant King speaking was becoming especially unpleasant. When he reached the entrance, Reed pulled the handbrake on and cut the engine.

He glanced over his shoulder then. "Be ready for anything, I guess."

"We don't have a plan?" Emma asked. The ute rocked as Diego hopped out.

"I don't think we can," Reed said. *A fact I don't really care for, to be honest.* "But I'm going to try Sonorous if we don't get very far, so be ready, guys."

"Right," Max said from outside.

Reed climbed out then drew his gun and then the bell before starting through the rows of cars at a stride. *Time to finish this somehow.* Once he did, he could get back to finding justice for Elise. He knew the truth now, even if he couldn't prove it, considering Phillip was gone. But that meant Dunstall was fair game now.

First, the Radiant King.

Between the cars and trucks he caught glimpses of a tall structure but it was still obscured for the moment. He slowed. The vehicles were thinning to be replaced by rows and rows of parking meters... and scarecrows! They stood in hats and coats, yellow tufts bright, in their own ring that encircled a steely throne.

At the foot of the throne were even more odd things

arranged to face the great seat; action figures and coffee mugs with novelty messages, bottle caps and colourful marbles.

Reed's confusion was swept away by the throne itself – the bottom appeared as a steely root system plunging into sand; they were both regular in shape and size like pipes, and also gnarled as a tree. Some were an uneven mix of both.

Before the actual seat there rested a small crystal chamber where a green, mulch-coloured hand with black nails leapt about like a restless spider. Trapped.

Higher up, waited the chair and its occupant.

The steel backing spread out in a towering thrust of uneven, jagged rays. Fitting for the Radiant King, who perched upon the seat like a bird of prey. His body was the same mix of untouched and burnt flesh and his face still blank, the crown still sharp.

But his legs and arms were elongated further now, trailing down to hanging from the throne, and when Reed neared, the neck extended to weave above them.

You are a Gift, My Lavender.

Reed. "I am not."

No, you are very much precisely that. For perhaps upon your own Plane you might continue to thwart me, especially with such stalwart allies, but not in my Kingdom.

Reed spun – Max, Lina, Diego and Emma had all turned to stone! Even with the wards of her symbol?

And so I thank you for accepting my invitation.

He lifted his gun. "Release them."

That will not stop me, Human.

"I'm not all human."

Even so. I am beyond any that you have encountered – it

would be best for you to submit. I will absorb you and then you might continue, after a fashion.

The sense of paper brushing against his skin began to change. It grew firmer, heavier, and at the same time, stinging, as though he was being sliced. Yet no blood welled. He clenched his jaw, steeling himself against it but the weight was unfathomable. He dropped to one knee as the invisible weight pressed upon his shoulders and even against his chest.

He could still move, however. Not well, but enough. *Am I turning to stone too?*

He raised the gun to level it at the Radiant King with a curse.

I have said, that will not succeed.

Reed managed to grin. "I'm going to try, anyway."

He dropped his arm a little then squeezed the trigger. The shot rang out and he jammed the trigger down again, emptying the chamber to the faint ring of crystal shattering.

Feronia's hand burst forth.

It hit the sand with a small puff and immediately, a sizzling sound rose up to meet the glittering fragments that continued to trickle from its cage.

A screech of rage rocked Reed's very core. It sent him sliding across the ground where he scattered marbles and plastic action figures alike, Sonorous and his gun knocked from his grip. The weight was even stronger now and he gasped for breath. Somehow, he managed to turn onto his back, only to see the Radiant King looming above him.

That was most *unwelcome, Mr Lavender.*

Reed clawed for a weapon – and found the hilt of the Gladius!

But could not draw it, so powerful was the pressure. The scent of burning sand overwhelmed his nose and throat, searing his eyes and he gagged at the taste of worm-flesh, even as darkness shrouded him.

Chapter 29.

Reed opened his eyes to a wealth of orange and yellow light, though it wavered slowly, as though he stood within a slowly flickering candle. But colour and faint shapes at the limits of his vision seemed like a dark honeycomb.

And he was standing now, instead of lying upon stone and debris before the Radiant King's throne and patch of sand.

The King was nowhere to be seen.

But another figure did share the strange place. A tall man, familiar... *Dad? Gods, is this real?*

His father looked the same as all those years ago; dark hair cut close, strong cheeks to go with his generally muscled physique – he was ex-army and never gave up on maintaining battle condition. *He'd always joked that he would never be able to keep Mum's attention otherwise.*

But that had just been a lie they'd used to tease each other.

Reed blinked back tears. *If only I could hear them again.* "Is this a trick?" he asked. His voice was swallowed by the warm glow.

"No, son," his father replied. His voice was deeper than Reed remembered, but it was the same.

Reed strode closer. It only took two steps, and then he'd caught his father in a hug, and real arms surrounded him, gave him a squeeze before pulling back to grip him by the shoulders. "Want me to tell you how much you've grown?" he said with a smile.

"Can we start with happened first?" Reed asked, somehow able to laugh in response. But his joy didn't last. "I'm sorry I didn't keep looking."

"Not even for a second did I blame you, and neither did your mother."

"Is she here too?"

"No; I don't know where she is either. I've been trapped within this thing since we were captured."

Reed nodded slowly. *Then Aunty and the other Gods weren't lying... they really didn't know what happened.* There was little time to feel remorse at his outburst. "Did you stumble across the Radiant King?"

"Yes, though his name, among others, is Enki."

"Enki... isn't that a Sumerian God?"

His father nodded. "Of wisdom and trickery among other things, and long thought Vanished. Your Mum found hints that he was stirring. Put simply, we got too close and I've been here ever since."

"So, are we inside Enki?"

"No, only one of his shells," his father said with a small frown. "When he captures humans he uses them as agents, and it's only me right now. He's *trying* to absorb you but I'm stopping him."

Reed stiffened. "We have to get out of here then."

"I can't."

"There has to be a way."

"Not that I have found so far," he replied. "And I'm running out of time, Reed. I'm sending you back but once I do, don't be shocked at what you see. *I'm* still here." Already he was beginning to fade into the smoky amber.

"Wait, what do you mean?"

"If you can find your mother, the two of you might just be able to get me out of here." His father was barely a glimpse now, though his voice remained clear.

"But where?"

"I don't know but you've got some time while Enki chases Feronia's hand; make sure you use it – I know you can do this, Reed."

"Dad!"

Bright blue sky above replaced the flame, that and pain from several things digging into Reed's back – marbles and action figures. He rose from where he lay. The sense of paper and worms had faded, but his friends were still sealed in stone within the amphitheatre.

Beside him, the ungainly form of the Radiant King waited... and the face was no longer blank.

Dad.

Reed had to look away. To see his father's face, older than when they'd just met, twisted into the Radiant King's body... But he had to look back, to make sure the shell was no longer a threat.

And clearly Enki was no longer using the grotesque body.

Its limbs were curled across the chest and ground, having scattered the ornaments, and the crown now seemed thinner, less a thing of terror. And above all, what Reed already knew, there was no overwhelming sense of the God's power.

He stood, a trembling breath escaping.

How many answers had he been given – only to have them buried by dozens of others? *Dad's not gone but he's trapped.* And his body had been taken all those years ago. Reed clenched a fist. Enki would pay for what he'd done, God or no. *To me and to everyone, like Patrick and the people from the train, and all the people I don't even know about yet.* "Somehow." The details of *how* weren't important.

The oath would have to be enough.

Maybe one thing made sense now, though it hardly seemed to matter: the spirit worms. *Whenever the Radiant King used Dad's body to abduct someone else, the worms formed.* Though that did create new questions. What was Enki collecting humans for? It hardly seemed he wanted to populate his strange towns... they were all empty. Yet, the King had some sort of goal, even with the childish nature to some of it.

Reed glanced back down at his father's unnatural face.

How close had his parents come to learning that goal? *And where's Mum now?* Looking for her would be impossible without more help than he'd been offered so far. *And if Dad is still contained within Enki, who could ever free him?*

This time, Aunty and the others would need to step up.

Being a pawn or a canary was only tolerable when there was a chance of achieving his own goals at the same time. He had more hope than before; his parents weren't simply Vanished, he had an answer. Something to follow-up on. There was a chance he'd be able to find them.

And maybe there was time to get ahead of Enki too, if he was busy chasing Feronia's hand? *That's what Dad told me at least.*

But two questions troubled him above the others.

First, Dad's totally human, so how did he stand up to the Radiant King and then get me out of there? Reed moved toward the frozen shapes of his friends, where he'd have to call Dionysus to help. *And finally, why the hell does a Sumarian God want* me *specifically?*

Chapter 30.

Somewhere, the Gods were gathering to plot and plan.

But for now, they'd left Reed and everyone else to make preparations. Whatever it was the Radiant King – or Enki – had built still needed exploring. Aunty had explained that the Sumerian's plane was beyond *and* between that of the Human and other Divine states of existence but the details remained unclear to Reed; that sort of thing had always been too esoteric.

And it was hard to stop his thoughts turning to his parents.

"Reed?"

Lina had left the others, who were still loading up the ute's tray with supplies – fuel, spare tyres, rope and explosives too, but chief among them, water from Dionysus' fountain. Emma was carrying a small keg and Diego lifted two to rest upon each shoulder.

"Max wanted me to accuse you of slacking off to break the ice; he likes to pretend that we all take his jokes seriously."

"Break the ice, huh?" he said with a small smile.

"Of your dark mood," she added.

He smiled. "I understood what he was going for, but I think I feel better than I have in years."

"Good." She hesitated.

"But?"

Lina spread her hands. "I just don't want you to get your hopes up. Everyone made it pretty clear that we're lucky to have escaped that mess back there."

"They're not wrong."

"Right, so what are you thinking? I know you're planning something, Reed."

"I'm planning to get to the bottom of this place, especially the nearby city Aunty mentioned, and hopefully find Patrick too. And then I'm going to hunt down Dunstall when we get back, even if he's still overseas."

"And then?"

He scratched at his head – still a little sandy. "Then Elise's family will get some peace or sense of justice, I hope."

"Then you're coming back here to go after Enki, I assume."

"Unless Jupiter has changed his mind, I don't think I have a choice," he said. "But I want to, yeah."

"Well, just so you know, you're still in jail."

He glanced at her, then chuckled. "Right."

"What's your plan for that problem?"

Reed sighed. "No idea, yet. Maybe the doll should stay put for a while longer."

"That's probably for the best," she said, rubbing at her jaw a moment. "Okay, I've got one more question, Reed."

"Hit me."

"What about Emma? You know she's the kind of person

who'll want to see this through."

"It's a good quality to have."

"That's not what I mean. She's *wholly* human; it's too dangerous."

"I don't feel that much safer being half-human, to be honest."

Lina gave his shoulder a punch. "I mean it. Minerva might ask Emma to help, and I want you to stop that from happening."

He frowned. "You're right about the danger. And Minerva may or may not allow Emma to help, but why are you pushing for this?"

"Because I like Emma, you idiot. I think she's good for you."

"I like her too," he replied. Despite the happy words, a creeping chill began to cross his shoulders. Lina's concern was not to be dismissed. But wasn't the safest place – for anyone – to be in the group that would be afforded the most power and attention from the gods? *Not that Emma needs me to tell her what to do.* "But I don't think it's up to me."

"Of course, but she might listen to you."

"Maybe."

Lina started back for the others. "Just think about it."

A Note from Ashley

Hi! I hope you enjoyed The Radiant King and thanks for reading.

I'd like to ask if you could help me out by leaving an honest review of the book at your place of purchase? Long or short, bad or good, it all helps!

AND if you'd like to sign up to my newsletter you'll be the first to know when the next Reed Lavender story is released. You'll also have first access to preview chapters and pre-release editions of the story, in addition to being automatically added into the draw for giveaways.

Ashley

ACKNOWLEDGMENTS

This time around I need to thank those of you who urged me to try my hand at an Urban Fantasy story! I'm having a lot of fun writing the Reed Lavender books. And of course, once more I want to thank Brooke for her constant support and belief in me!

Also, to everyone who works hard to help me at every stage of the process, but especially once more to Rebekah at VividCovers for yet another great cover.

Ashley Capes

www.ingramcontent.com/pod-product-compliance
Lightning Source LLC
Chambersburg PA
CBHW030649110726
47901CB00002B/641